One Night
and Other Stories

Chris Gonnerman

Table of Contents

One Night in Slateholm

Chapter 1: Within The Tower

They say the city of Slateholm never sleeps, but no one took note of me as I slipped into an alleyway in the Merchant's Quarter. It was dark, just before midnight, and the waning moon had not yet risen. My soft boots made no sound on the cobblestones of the alley. I was armored in dark leather with dull metal studs, in hopes of going unnoticed.

The narrow alley *zigged* to the left, then *zagged* to the right, so that no one looking from one end would be able to see through to the other. At the first turning I reached my left hand over my shoulder and drew my four-foot blade from its scabbard. The blade was dull black metal; only the edges shone.

Thus prepared I continued slinking quietly through the darkness. At the second turning I could see the magical light which illuminated my target: the huge, squat tower at the end of the alley, around which the alley broke to the left and right like a stream breaking around a rock. Though it was called a tower, the great pile was well over a hundred feet across but no more than fifty feet high. No windows pierced it at ground level, and no upper-floor windows were visible from the back. The only way in from the back was a single door, up three steps from street level.

For a moment I stopped... I smelled a faint, pleasant scent over the foul smells of rotting garbage and excrement filling the alleyway. But it was gone as soon as I noticed it; shaking my head, I moved on, approaching the tower but staying out of the light. For a while I stood still, studying the doorway. Getting inside was going to be a challenge, but I had come prepared.

With my right hand I fished a small phial from my beltpouch, opened it and swallowed the contents. Its taste was as unpleasant as the last time I had used it; grimacing, I restored the phial to its hiding place. Without further delay I approached the door and knocked, then quickly hunkered down against it. The small peephole in the door opened with a squeal, but of course the guard within could not see me; after a few moments it closed. I reached up and knocked again, and the peephole opened more quickly. "Who's there?" said a guttural voice. Receiving no answer, the guard within closed the peephole again, and yet again I knocked.

This time I felt the door opening behind me. Before it could open more than a crack, I said loudly, "What do you think you're doing?" Thanks to the magic of the potion I had drunk, my voice came from within the tower rather than from my own mouth.

I heard his heavy boots as he turned and took a few steps toward the sound of my voice, and thus away from me, and even as he said, "What? Who's there?" I leaped to my feet and shoved the door the rest of the way open. The chainmail-clad guard within was looking away, down the darkened corridor toward my voice. He was already beginning to turn to face me, having heard the door open, but before he could complete the maneuver I brought my weapon down two-handed across his neck.

The guard fell, making two distinct thuds as he struck the stone floor. I looked down for a moment on my fallen foe, who it seemed was not a man but a hobgoblin. Then I smelled it again, and I muttered "Jasmine?" under my breath.

I quietly closed the outer door and lowered the bar into place. The hallway was unlit, but I could see light illuminating a door at the far end. Feeling my way to the end of the corridor, I noted several doors along the way, all apparently locked; but when I tried the door at the end, it was unlocked. So I carefully opened it, a crack at first, then enough to pass through into the large chamber beyond.

The room was circular, perhaps sixty feet in diameter, and opulently decorated. It was illuminated magically, as I expected, and the light was sourceless; looking down, I saw that I cast no shadow. The wall was lined with single doors, with an ornate pair of double doors on the far side. The ceiling was a dome, perhaps fifty feet to the top, painted black and set with glowing gemstone stars. But it was the staircase that attracted my attention.

A well of sorts, almost thirty feet across, dominated the room. The well had neither wall nor railing around it, but was merely a gaping hole in the floor. A spiral staircase descended around the outside of the well. There was no light within, save apparently at the very bottom, so the staircase was rather gloomy. It looked all the more dangerous because it also had no railing.

I heard a scuffling noise on the stone-flagged floor behind me, and I turned swiftly to discover four more hobgoblins behind me. "Trying to sneak up on me?" I said, smiling grimly. They just smiled back, displaying their prominent lower tusks. As we advanced, I reached down with my right hand and drew a long dirk from a scabbard in my boot.

They fell upon me then, swinging heavy maces, and with my good black sword in my left hand and the dirk in my right, I wove a virtual web of steel around myself, fending them off. Still, I knew while I held the hobgoblins at bay, I would not be able to strike back at them without leaving myself open to attack. I knew it was only a matter of time before I would fall before their rain of blows.

Suddenly, one of the hobgoblins fell. The others were surprised, and one turned to see what had become of his comrade, so I took advantage of the situation, burying my dirk in the distracted hobgoblin's side.

A slim feminine figure joined the fight; the blood on her dagger made it obvious it was she who laid the first one low. Now, with the odds suddenly even, my fighting grin returned. I turned the full force of both of my weapons against one hobgoblin while the other turned to fight the woman.

Shortly I landed a fatal blow with my sword, felling my opponent. The woman was backing away, dodging and parrying the hobgoblin, who seemed unaware that he was now alone. I stole up behind him and ended his life with my dirk.

We stood there a moment, breathing hard, and I regarded the woman. She was clad in a dark cloak over leather armor. Finally I said, "I'm John Northcrosse."

"Call me Eldritch," she replied.

"Not your real name."

"Not your business," she said, a defiant grin on her face.

"You're a half-elf," I said. "You've the ears and eyes of an elf, but the curves of a woman. And you wear jasmine perfume."

"You're observant, for a human," she replied, and I smiled. "Come," she continued, her tone changing, "we are here for the same reason, I'm sure, and we make a good team. Let's continue together."

I frowned. "The last comrades-in-arms I had lie buried in a temple in the desert of Nol. I was the only survivor."

"I'm not worried," she said, smiling broadly.

"Very well," I replied. "You were invisible before... can you be so again?"

"My ring must rest a while first, I'm afraid," she replied.

"I see. Well, it seems we must descend. Ladies first?"

"Chivalry?" she said, grinning. "Just this one time, why don't you lead?"

"Very well," I said again, wiping my bloody weapons on the cloak of the nearest fallen foe. I turned to the stair and began downward, following the wall and staying well clear of the rail-less inner edge. Eldritch followed close behind me.

We descended three full times around before reaching the bottom of the shaft, entering the magical illumination at the bottom cautiously. Just as we reached it, the clatter of armored men, or perhaps more hobgoblins, came from above. "They're behind us," I said quietly. "There's a doorway there, at the foot of the steps, we should try to get through it before they see us."

"No," whispered the half-elf. "Under the steps is a better place. There's only one doorway here, so it must be their destination. I'd rather be behind them than in front of them."

I nodded my assent, and took a quick look up. "Now, let's move, I don't think they'll see us."

It was hobgoblins, I saw, peeking carefully out from beneath the stairs, and there were five of them. They went directly to the door and passed through, though the last one did stop and glance around the well-bottom; but I foresaw his movement and drew back beneath the stair, and we went undiscovered.

After a few moments of silence, I stepped out from under the stairs. I looked around, but did not see Eldritch. "Your ring has rested, eh?" I said.

"Yes," came her disembodied voice.

"Good. They may come back this way, when they don't find us beyond. If they do, I'll draw them in here, and you try to get behind them."

"Aye, it worked once, it may well work again," she replied.

I quietly walked to the doorway; beyond the half-open doors, I saw a passageway, perhaps twenty feet wide with a ten foot ceiling. Every twenty feet or so, a heavy dolmen arch made of stones three feet thick supported the ceiling. "Very good," I whispered, "I can use these arches for cover." With that, I moved quickly down the darkened corridor, beckoned onward by a set of double doors outlined thinly with light at the far end.

As I approached the doors, I heard a soft male voice from the lighted space beyond. "I'm very disappointed in you," said the voice, "letting thieves into my house."

"Master, please," said a harsh yet quiet voice, "Grak and Og and the others, they were weak and stupid. We'll find the thieves and kill them for you."

"No," came the soft voice in reply, "stay here. I don't trust you to keep the thieves away from me. No telling what trouble they might cause, and I'm rather busy right now. Go back to the stairs and stand guard."

Hearing that, I quickly took cover behind one of the arch-pillars. "Damn, this won't do," I whispered fiercely, "they'll see me for sure." But no answer came... if Eldritch was near me, she didn't answer.

Then suddenly I remembered my potion, and wondered if it might still be working. As the doors behind me opened, I yelled "Damn, they're coming, back up the stairs!" I thanked whichever of the Hundred Gods governed the powers of magic when my voice came not from my mouth, but from far down the passage toward the stairs. Sure enough, hearing that the hobgoblins broke into a run and never looked back, passing just inches from me without noticing.

I stepped out of my hiding place, looked briefly toward the hobgoblins, and then turned the other way. They had left the doors half-open; through them, I could see a large, softly illuminated room, and a man in elaborately-decorated robes facing away from me.

The man, it turned out, was standing before a sort of stone table or altar. Around him I could see the slim hands and feet of a bound victim, the rest of her body being hidden by his large belly. Without turning, the robed man said softly, "Come in, come in."

I was startled, but only for the briefest moment. "So, Pentalion, the rumors are true... you do engage in human sacrifice."

"Sacrifice?" said the large man, turning. "I suppose you could call it that. But I won't harm a hair on her head." He stepped aside so that I could see the victim's face, but my eyes were following the wicked knife in his right hand. "Oh, this?" he said, seeing John's gaze. "I was merely going to remove her gag."

I turned my gaze on the victim, clad only in a light night-dress. With her eyes she begged my aid. "She's just a girl," I said.

"Why, my friend," replied Pentalion, smiling wickedly, "when you must choose your virgins from among the population of the Poor Quarter, they're apt to be a mite young."

I hefted my sword and began to advance on the robed man, but he said *"Laflictis"*, and with arms upraised he flew up into the air.

"You think I can't harm you simply because you are out of reach of my sword?" I said, drawing my dirk; but even as I did so, Pentalion said *"Dephlotis"* and made a dismissing gesture with his hands. When I threw the weapon it turned aside in midair, falling harmlessly to the floor.

Pentalion smiled. "You see," he said, still speaking softly, "you cannot harm me. But I, on the other hand... *solectu!*" A blue-white bolt of lightning struck down from the wizard's outstretched hands. I leapt aside, but the twisting, arcing bolt grazed me, throwing me to the flagstones.

I lay there for a moment, stunned and twitching. As soon as I could, I picked up my sword and began to rise. "I have more," said the wizard in his soft voice.

Then I heard another voice, feminine, speak the word *"Interecti"*, and suddenly Pentalion fell to the floor, crying out when he hit; the sharp sound of his impact signaled a broken bone. Smiling grimly, I stepped forward again, grasped my sword in both hands and raised it high.

Pentalion looked up, in obvious pain, and said *"Thalactis."* With a sickening twist his body seemed to collapse and disappear. "He's teleported," said Eldritch. "No telling where he's gone."

"Free her," I replied, "while I look for him." I turned toward the exit just in time to see the doors slam shut, and before I could reach them I heard a bar slam down. "Damn, we're going to have to work to get those open."

Turning, I saw that Eldritch had freed the girl. I began to walk back to them, but even as I did, a huge, eyeless head reared up behind the stone table. Its neck was long and serpentine, its skin was pasty white and slimy, and its open mouth was lined with hundreds of long, sharp teeth. "Look out!" I yelled.

Eldritch turned and saw her peril, and grabbing the girl, she leapt out of the way as the monster struck swiftly, snakelike. I wasted no time, running forward and burying my sword to the hilt in the monster's neck.

For a moment, all was quiet. I pulled my sword out of the monstrous creature's flesh and stepped back. "Is it dead?" asked the girl in a small voice.

As if in answer, the creature rose up and shook itself, and as it did, four identical heads joined it from behind the table. "There's a pit back there," said Eldritch, dodging away from a strike. "That's where the creatures are coming from."

"I don't think it's 'creatures,'" I replied, dodging. "I think it's one creature. Some kind of hydra." One of the heads struck at me, and I dodged aside. I struck at the serpentine neck as it passed me, scoring a solid hit, but the wound seemed to close almost as soon as I drew back my sword.

The heads began striking in earnest, two or three at a time, and it was all we could do to avoid them. I struck at it here and there, but my mightiest blow seemed to do the monster no real harm. "What do we have to do to kill this damned thing?" I yelled in frustration.

Finally I had a moment to breathe as all the heads drew back at the same time, and I looked for the girl. After a brief moment I found her, crouching near the door and crying softly, seemingly unharmed.

Eldritch looked also, and her face lit up. As she dodged another attack she called out, "They can't see us, John, they must be hearing us."

"Hearing us," I mused, and then I began yelling, "Over here, you stupid frog-snakes! Come and get me!" I was using the magic of the potion, which thankfully was still in effect, to cast my voice behind the monster. The monster's heads turned as one to attack my phantom voice, smashing uselessly into the wall.

Still yelling to draw its attention, I slowly moved over to the stone table, and saw behind it the monster's body within the pit. It was, as I had suspected, a single monster, five heads attached to a single massive body. Reversing my sword and taking it in both hands, I leaped into the pit and thrust it between the heads with my full weight, driving it deep into the body.

The monster's death throes were prodigious, and I was smashed against the wall of the pit and knocked unconscious. The next thing I heard was the voice of Eldritch, calling down to me. I shook myself, then sat up. I was drenched in the monster's foul blood but apparently not too badly harmed. "Need a hand, friend?" Eldritch asked, smiling broadly.

"In a moment," I said, standing up and checking my limbs. Turning to the gory carcass, I grabbed my sword. It took me several tries to pull it out, and by that time, Eldritch had made a silk rope fast to the stone table. I wiped my weapon on my blood-fouled cloak as best I could, sheathed it and climbed out of the pit.

"You need a bath, John Northcrosse," said Eldritch. "And your gear could use one too."

I just smiled at her. "Have you any magic to open the doors?"

"I think so," she replied. She laid her hands on the doors and said *"fralineen,"* and I heard the bar fly from the other side and land with a crash. I led the way out, and Eldritch followed, guiding the girl.

We met the hobgoblins at the foot of the stair, but the sight of the blood-soaked swordsman raising his dripping sword to oppose them was too much even for such brutish creatures... they turned and ran up the stairs as fast as they could. I laughed grimly as I trudged up the stairs.

Suddenly I heard a rumbling noise, and the stairway shuddered. "The steps, they're moving!" said Eldritch.

"They're pulling back into the wall," I replied. "We'll have to move fast if we want to get up there before they're gone." With that, I began to run up the steps, taking them two at a time.

Eldritch said *"laflictis,"* and rose into the air, carrying the girl. "I'll meet you at the top," she said as she passed me.

I just kept running, and the steps kept getting narrower. I had to slow to a walk, face against the wall, to make it the last few steps. When at last my hands could reach the top of the well, I pulled myself out.

Eldritch and the girl were indeed waiting. "Look," said the girl, and I turned toward the well. It was closing up, shrinking somehow. Soon there was no sign it had ever been there.

"Swordsman!" came the voice of the wizard. He was seated on a chair, framed in the now-open double doorway at the front of the room. Behind him stood the five hobgoblins, weapons at the ready but looking nervous. "Swordsman," he said again, "you have won this round. Leave by the back entrance. A messenger has already been sent to fetch the watch... if you are still here when they come, you'll be arrested."

"We'll meet again," I said, motioning for Eldritch and the girl to precede me.

"Count on it," replied the wizard, his eyes sharply glinting. "Count on it..."

Chapter 2: Eldritch's Hideout

"What's your name, girl?" Eldritch asked after we were outside.

"M-Marisa, if it please you, m'lady," replied the girl in a small voice.

"Please don't speak thus to me, Marisa. I was a poor girl once too, and still as common as water." The girl shivered, and Eldritch threw her cloak around her shoulders. "We will escort you home if you will let us."

"Y-Yes, I would I-like that," she said, and so Eldritch took the girl by the hand, and I followed them to a tenement in the Poor Quarter. Considering my rather frightful condition, drenched in the mixed blood and slime of the strange hydra, I remained in the shadows of an alley while Eldritch saw to Marisa's return home.

When Eldritch returned, she said, "Where are you staying, John Northcrosse?"

"I've been renting a room at the Medusa's Mirror for a few weeks now."

"Ah," she said. "It seems, if I remember rightly, that they do not have a bathhouse. You'll be obliged to pay for the privilege of being clean."

"So it seems," I replied.

"It happens that I have a bathtub, and a well, and means for heating the water. If you wish, you may make use of them for free."

"I see," I said, looking at Eldritch with new eyes. Was this mere compassion, or did she wish to court me, or perhaps even bed me? She was young, perhaps fifteen years at most, with the curves of womanhood still reaching for full flower... attractive, but younger than I would have liked. For my own part, after the loss of my comrades in Nol I was in no hurry to form any strong attachments.

"You are very kind," I said after a moment, "and I could use a good cleaning. If you do not fear for your reputation, that is."

"I do not," she replied, "for no one will see us."

"How so?"

"Hide your light and I will guide us." I had forgotten for a moment that she was of half elven blood, and thus could see in the dark. I was wearing a copper coin enchanted with a long-lasting spell of light to illuminate my travels, for the Poor Quarter is largely unlit after nightfall.

I did as she bid me, removing the coin on its chain from my neck and tucking it into my pouch. As soon as I pulled the drawstring tight, we were plunged into near total darkness; above me I could see a few stars, but the moon had not yet risen.

"Here, give me your hand," she said, and I removed the befouled glove from my right hand and reached out. I was surprised when she grasped it... her hand was soft, not remarkable for woman, elf, or wizard, all of which was part of her being, but it was also stronger than I would have expected. I could feel confidence in her grip. As she led me off, I tucked the glove into my belt so my hand would be free to draw sword or dirk at need.

We wandered, or so it seemed to me, for quite a while, and from the smells and the occasional things squishing underfoot I gathered we were keeping to the alleys. Eldritch was sure-footed and careful, and never led me through any place my feet would not pass. Unfortunately, she forgot how much taller I was than she, and guided me past a low hanging... something... a bar or beam or branch, I knew not what, only that it did not give when the top of my head struck it.

I resisted the urge to cry out or curse, though I'm sure some sound escaped my lips. Eldritch stopped, and I felt her fingers gliding over the top of my head. "Sorry," she whispered, "I'll be more careful."

I nodded, assuming that she could see the motion, and after a moment she started again. It wasn't much farther before she stopped again. "Wait," she whispered, releasing my hand, and shortly I heard a soft grating sound of wood on stone. "Come," she said, taking my hand again. "There are four steps up."

After I had entered the structure, I heard the sound again, and then she said, "You may use your light now." I withdrew the coin and found us in a narrow curving passageway in a musty wooden building; a door lay in front of me, while behind me was the rickety-looking door through which we entered. The passageway became a staircase leading downward to my left, and upward to my right. Eldritch turned right and preceded me up the staircase.

We arrived at a place with a trapdoor above us, which she opened. The room beyond was a circular attic, with a most peculiar interior shape... it was like being inside an onion. A doorknob, of all things, hung from the highly-peaked center of the ceiling by a bit of rope and illuminated the room by magic. A number of cloth hangings hung on a rope divided the space in two, with the hangings being just a bit above my eye level. The half of the space I could see included the promised bathtub, a washstand with a mirror, a chamberpot-cabinet beside it, and a comfortable-looking but threadbare chair. A few mismatched rugs lay on the floor. I could see two low windows, covered with heavy fabric; from their placement I guessed at two more behind the partition.

Eldritch threw her cloak over the chair; underneath she wore a dark green silk shirt, fitted but not tight, pants of soft black leather cut the same way, and high soft leather boots the color of slate. She turned and looked at me, and I regarded her in turn... striking green elvish eyes set in a girlish face framed with long black hair that didn't quite hide her pointed ears. She was a little more than five feet in height, and I felt as if I towered over her, but I could tell my size did not intimidate her at all.

"I sleep beyond the hangings," she said. "Please wait here, and I will start the water heating." With that, she parted the hangings and passed through. I took the time to remove my boots and my armor, keeping the slightly soiled padded undershirt and breeches on in service to my modesty. I heard her busying herself, and after a few moments she returned, bearing a bucket of water and a handful of rags. "You can clean your armor with this," she said. "I have oil for the leather when you are done. By then, perhaps the water will be hot enough."

Then she left me again, and so I sat down on the rugs and began working on my armor. I had oiled it pretty well the last time I tended to it, which made removing the sticky dark orange blood of the monster easier than it might have been.

It took Eldritch two passes with a bucket and a battered cauldron full of hot water before the tub contained enough to bathe in. I said, "Sorceress, I have put you to quite a bit of trouble tonight. How can I repay you?"

"Get in the water before it gets cold," she replied. As she left once again through the partition, she said, "Later perhaps you can make a few trips to the well in the basement and refill my barrel."

I felt somewhat more human after a good hot bath, the aches of the night's battle washed away with the hot water. As I stood at the mirror afterward, I noticed that my skin was still dark and my hair pale, the signs of my adventures in Nol; I also noticed that I looked as haggard as though I had been on a three day drunk, my hair wild and my beard disreputable. I could have waited until morning, sought out a barber and got a proper cut, but for the moment I decided to trim my beard and tie my overlong hair back.

Rummaging through the cabinet below the washstand, I found scissors, but as usual they were made for a right-handed person; I could not make them work. It was then that I heard a sound behind me, and I turned and found Eldritch standing there.

"Let me help you with that," she said, ignoring the fact that I was naked but for a cloth wrapped around my hips. I decided, if she were not embarrassed, neither would I be.

"You are too kind, m'lady," I said, taking a seat upon the chamberpot-cabinet and handing her the scissors. As she set to work on my hair, I said, "You are brave, you know," I said. "Or foolish, some might say. I am a foreign warrior, a barbarian even, whom you know but little, yet you welcomed me into your hiding place at our first meeting."

"You should not call someone foolish who is standing behind you with scissors," she said, and I laughed mock-ruefully. "I knew I could trust you," she continued. "I am a good judge of men."

"Indeed," I said, not entirely convinced.

She frowned intently at me. "You went into the lair of a powerful wizard alone, or so you thought, to try to rescue a child whose name and parentage were unknown to you. This speaks of your honor, more than any oath or vow might." She paused a moment, then went on, "In the well, when you wanted to precede the hobgoblins through the door, I offered another plan which you immediately accepted."

"Hiding under the stairs seemed a far better plan than mine," I replied. "I'd have been a fool not to do as you said."

"I'm glad you are no fool," she said, moving around to trim my beard. "Still, I am not accustomed to a man who values my opinion. I'm not sure I know any others, in fact. Are all the men of your village like you?"

"I doubt it," I replied, smiling broadly. "Most men fear a woman with an opinion, and what you fear, you try to prevent. But I am John Northcrosse! I have fought men and monsters from the Demonfrost Mountains to the Desert of Nol. I have won a drinking contest with a dwarf, and a debate with an elf, and I have eaten the heart of a dragon. Why then would I be afraid of a woman with an opinion?"

I was expecting at least a grin, if not a laugh, but Eldritch was wearing an expression of simmering disapproval. "What was that?" she asked, gesturing with the scissors in an irritated fashion.

"What was what?" I asked.

"That. 'I am John Northcrosse,' and so on. I do not care for a man who brags."

My face fell. "Dear sorceress," I said, "among my people, when two men duel, they begin by boasting of their prowess, of the men and beasts they have vanquished. The first time I did that in the company of my former comrades, they found my barbaric ways hilarious. I could have become angry and sulked about it, but instead I decided to make it a jest. I began to boast of defeating a horde of rampaging squirrels, or standing fearless in the face of a tonguelashing by my foeman's mother. In that way, my friends and I could laugh while our foemen, convinced that the joke was somehow on them, would become careless in their anger. The boast I just made is the last one I spoke in company with my friends."

"I see," she said, still with a note of disapproval.

"I have not boasted thusly in many weeks," I continued. "That I have remembered mirth after so long is surely a good thing, is it not?"

"Yes, of course," she said, her mood brightening suddenly. Remembering herself then, she finished with my beard and moved around me again, cutting a bit here and there as she went. At last, she brushed the hair from my shoulders and said, "How is that?"

I turned and looked in the mirror; the man who looked back at me was quite presentable, and I said, "Very good, thank you. You could be a barber."

"I've been many things," she replied, and I felt her hand on my shoulder.

I stood up then and turned toward her. "Eldritch, if you are making an overture toward me, please know I do not take advantage of young and innocent girls."

She laughed then. "Innocent? That's a matter for later discussion. But young, now... have you any idea how old I am, swordsman?"

"I'd wager fifteen years," I replied.

She laughed again. "This will be my twenty-seventh winter," she replied. "You forget I am half elven. How old are you?"

"Twenty-one," I replied, sheepishly.

"Well, John Northcrosse, please know I do not take advantage of young and innocent boys."

I grinned at her turn of my phrase, then said, "Innocent? That's a matter for later discussion," and we both had a good laugh, though I still wondered at her intentions. I had taken her for fifteen, but had not considered the youthful appearance of a half-elven woman, even though I should have known better. I decided to wait for a more tangible indication of her intentions.

The room had been chilly when I arrived, but by the time I had washed my undergarments in the cooling bath water and hung them on hooks which Eldritch pointed out to me, it was quite warm. "I only use the fireplace at night," she said, "putting it out well before daylight so that none see the smoke."

"This is not merely your home, then, but your hideout. What sort of place is it?"

She grinned at me. "It is an abandoned temple of a minor god," she replied. "Those who live nearby think it haunted, and sometimes I help them to believe that. The entrance we used is in an alley and appears boarded over, but is merely held with a hidden catch, so that I can come and go as I please."

"Abandoned temple?" I replied, a bit shocked. "Are you not concerned that staying here blasphemes the god, who might take offense and afflict you with some curse?"

"No," she said grimly. "I've known many curses. They do not concern me."

Though I was still a bit rattled by this disclosure, I decided, as I was nearly naked, my clothes were wet, and it was still dark and cold outside, that running screaming into the darkness was not a good plan. So instead I said, "Speaking of curses, what of Pentalion? Surely he will make some attempt on our lives."

"I would plan on it, John Northcrosse," she replied.

"Please, just call me John. We are comrades now, are we not?" She smiled faintly, then looked away as if distracted. "So we must make preparations, then."

"No," she said, "there is no point. All we can do is be on our guard. I do not have the magic to ward us from one as powerful as he. It was sheer luck my counterspell worked against him... it might easily have failed."

"I see," I said.

"It is late," she said. "If you'd like to stay here until morning, you may sleep on the rugs. I'm afraid I have only one bed, but I do have a spare blanket I can lend you."

"I'll do that, if you don't mind," I replied. So I laid my sword in its scabbard on the rugs, stretching out beside it under the threadbare blanket she lent me. Eldritch covered the glowing doorknob with a drawstring pouch, plunging the room into darkness, and shortly I fell into a deep, dreamless sleep.

Chapter 3: Pursuit and Evasion

I awakened at a touch, leaping to my feet and drawing my sword in one movement. It was Eldritch,

I saw, and she leaped backward into the hangings as quickly as I stood up.

Of course, I had been sleeping naked. Fortunately, Eldritch had become entangled in the hangings as she fled, giving me a moment to realize my situation and pick up the blanket. "Damn, woman, are you trying to get yourself killed? Sneaking up on a warrior who sleeps with his sword is not a healthy habit."

She laughed as she disentangled herself from the hangings. "I'm sorry, John Northcrosse. Next time I'll call your name from a distance." Her expression turned from mirth to seriousness suddenly. "It is less than an hour until dawn. I'd prefer you to return to your lodgings before then. Your clothing should be dry by now."

"Indeed," I said, laying my sword down but holding the blanket around me with one hand. "Do you wish me gone so quickly?"

Her face softened just a bit. "No. Like it or not, we have made an enemy of the same wizard; it would be best for us if we worked together, at least for a while. But I'm sure you left property at the Medusa's Mirror, and there at least you have a good bed to sleep in."

"Yes, I see what you mean. How are we to meet again, if you do not wish me to come here in daylight?"

"I will meet you at your inn at noontime, and we can plan our strategy then. I can leave here invisible in daylight without giving away my hideout, as you called it, but I do not have the magic to allow you to do the same."

"Noon it is, then," I replied. Eldritch returned beyond the hangings as I dressed, then preceded me down the steps to operate the secret catch on the door. I tried to see how she did it, but her hand moved too quickly to follow.

"Hide your light before I open the door, swordsman," she said. "Follow the curving wall on your left until it becomes straight; about ten more of your paces forward, and you may use your light without giving me away."

I complied with her instructions, and found myself on a nameless street when I took out the glowing coin. I turned and examined the abandoned temple so I would know it again later. On its doors were large circular medallions embossed with some sort of octopus or kraken.

I knew little of the city, a fact that Eldritch did not seem to have considered, but fortunately I was able to see enough of the sky to find my way by the stars until I crossed a familiar street. By the time I saw the snake-encircled metal disk that was the inn's sign, it was nearly dawn and a few people were on the streets.

The innkeeper met me in the common room of the inn. "Northman! Early this morning when all sensible men are asleep, guardsmen came knocking at my door and awakened me. They said the wizard Pentalion had identified you as a murderer and thief. I told them I didn't expect to see you again."

He was standing in my way, an expectant look on his face, so I reached into my beltpouch and pulled out a large emerald. "I appreciate your discretion."

"I thought you might," he replied, making it disappear faster than a street magician. "I'm sorry you have to go."

"Go?"

"I told them you were gone," he said, as he walked backward out of the common room. "I didn't say they believed me."

"Damn," I said, running up the stairs to my room. It was not a large room, but I had spread my possessions all over it... plate-and-mail armor, shortbow and quiver of arrows, riding boots, several changes of clothing, traveling pack, and other things too numerous to list. Discarded in the corner of the room was a small beer keg, which I quickly snatched up; pushing in and twisting the tap a quarter turn, I released the secret door in it and removed the folded silk within.

I shook out the black silk bag and opened it, then threw in the small keg, followed by my armor, boots, traveling pack, and everything else of value in the room. When I was done the only portable items left in the room were a few empty wine bottles and the cheap candleholder the innkeeper provided.

I pulled the silver drawstring on the magical bag, which weighed only a tenth part of its contents, and threw it over my shoulder. Turning about, I opened the door to leave.

I found myself face-to-face with a party of men in the livery of the city watch. I had caught them off guard, one with hand upraised to knock, another with his mouth open about to speak, and two more who simply looked surprised. I slammed the door in their faces, then turned and launched myself through the shuttered (but thankfully glass-free) window.

The shutters burst open when my shoulder met them, and I rolled out onto the rooftop which lay outside the window. I got to my feet and saw several more watchmen on the street below. They were surprised by my sudden appearance, giving me time to make a running leap to the rooftop of the next building. I was able to cross that building to the next street, and I knew the watchmen would need time to run through the alley to get to me. Swinging down to a balcony, I said, "Good morning," to a woman in a low-cut nightdress who was airing her bedding there, then swung over the railing to the ground before she could cry out for help.

Unfortunately, cry out she did, yelling to the pursuing watchmen, "There! He's gone down the alley! He's a pervert, cut his balls off!"

I spent the next few minutes running through the deeply-shadowed streets, thankful for the taller buildings of the Merchant's Quarter. There were still few people on the streets, which meant no crowds to hide me nor to slow down the watchmen.

It was then that I reached the canal. By decree of the Prince of Slateholm, the buildings were kept back from the canal, leaving a broad stripe unshadowed. Worse, the nearest bridge over the canal arched high enough to make me an excellent target. There was nothing to do but run, and run I did, zigging and zagging as much as I could to avoid the crossbow bolts I was sure would strike me at any moment.

I was counting myself lucky when I made it to the far side of the bridge, and I risked a look behind me. It was then that I was hit... a bolt launched from the far side of the canal went through my right shoulder. It didn't hurt immediately, due I was sure to my concentration on fleeing, but I knew I couldn't depend on it.

I ran into the narrow streets of the Poor Quarter, dodging into alleys and taking every possible turning in hopes of losing my pursuers. I knew they had me outnumbered, and if they were clever enough to split up they were sure to find me. Already injured, I did not stand much of a chance should I face more than one of them. I had little hope of reaching Eldritch, for I did not really know the way to the abandoned temple through the unfamiliar streets of Slateholm. My only chance was to find some nook in which to hide and wait for them to pass me by... but a man more than six feet in height carrying a large black silk bag and a four foot blade is hard to hide.

It didn't look good for me. As I ran, I said a quiet prayer under my breath. I felt sure I would be meeting the comrades I left in Nol very soon indeed, but I would go only after showing the watchmen the true mettle of a warrior of the northlands.

I turned a corner into a narrow street and nearly tripped over a one-legged beggar. "Pardon," I said. Then I had a thought, and reached into my beltpouch. My right shoulder chose that moment to remind me of the bolt still embedded in it, but I managed to find a gold crown in my pouch in spite of the pain. Letting him see it, I said, "Can you tell me how to find the abandoned temple with the krakens on the doors? I'm to meet a friend in a nearby alley."

He grinned at me toothlessly. "Aye, stranger. Go yonder there past the stonecutter's, and take the fourth turning to the right, then follow that street to the third left. You can't miss it." I tossed him the coin and took his directions. I turned right in the place he prescribed and found myself face-to-face with a watchman.

There seemed only one choice, so I lowered my good left shoulder and kept running. Fortune was with me for once as I caught him off-balance and bowled him over. This time I was smart enough not to look back until I rounded the next corner, where I risked it and caught a glimpse of the watchman more than a block behind me. I looked ahead and saw no sign of the temple; I knew if I continued very far, the watchman would catch sight of me again, so I ducked into the open front of a greengrocer's shop.

"Here now," said an old woman, "you can't be running through here!" Indeed, it was rather difficult to slip between the closely-spaced displays of vegetables, though I'm sure that wasn't exactly what she meant.

I reached painfully into my pouch for another gold crown, and throwing it to the woman, I said, "You haven't seen me."

"No, m'lord," she replied, grinning like a gargoyle.

It was dark within the shop, and I was still dazzled from the morning sun, so I said, "Have you a back door?" She pointed, and without further comment I made my way through it, into the narrow, curving alley behind the shop.

I chose to go right, but was pulled up short by my magical bag. It took me the briefest moment to discover that the drawstring was caught somehow on the back door of the greengrocer's. It was hard to see anything in the deeply shadowed alley, and I realized that I would likely not be able to free the bag in time.

I had no choice but to leave it behind.

I ran down the alley, hoping to become lost enough that the watchmen couldn't find me. My shoulder ached terribly, and every footstep I took made it throb with pain. Then I heard voices... "Hurry up, he's down here," came one voice, and "Out of my way, peasant," said another, and I knew my pursuers were closing in.

It was then that I came to an intersection, and realized I was behind the abandoned temple. I had found the place I was looking for... was I in time? I ran to the boarded-over rear door and pounded on it.

There was no answer. I tried to figure out the secret catch, but it was secret, after all, and I could not. Finally, expecting that I was done for, I put my back against the wall and drew my sword. I had heard much of what went on in the jails of Slateholm... I would go down fighting instead, and take some of them with me.

"What are you doing?" came the voice of Eldritch, whispering in my ear.

"Watchmen are after me," I replied. "Let me in!" The door opened, and I practically fell into the dimness beyond. Eldritch was obliged to stand over me to secure the door, and we held our poses as we heard the muffled voices of the watchmen outside. I could only hope they hadn't seen me... but when I heard them trying the door, I worried that they had. Keeping silent was the only thing to do.

After a few moments which felt like an hour, I heard another voice outside yelling, "This way! He's trying to make it to the gate!" and then I heard booted feet running away.

Eldritch carefully stepped over me, and I painfully dragged myself to my feet. Though the corridor was in near total darkness, she said softly, "You're hurt."

"Indeed," I replied quietly.

"Come, I'll tend to it," she said, and I heard her ascending the stairs. Getting my coin from my beltpouch was too painful to consider, so I sheathed my sword and attempted the stairs blind. I went slowly, and made it to the top just as she opened the trap door.

I sat on the chamberpot-cabinet again as I had the night before. "You'll have to pull it out backwards," I said. "It's too short to break it first."

"I don't want to hurt you," she replied.

"I've suffered it before." I awkwardly took the dirk from my right boot with my left hand, and placed the hilt between my teeth.

Eldritch took hold of the bolt in both hands, bracing her knee against my back, and said, "Ready?" Before I could nod, she pulled mightily and it came out. I bit down hard on my dirk to keep from crying out.

Eldritch stepped in front of me then, and I saw that my blood had splattered her face and hair. She took a rag from the washstand and wiped her face with it, then opened the cabinet below and reached far into the back, pulling out a small jar with a wide mouth. "This will help," she said, showing me the bluish salve inside.

"Magic?" I said, and she nodded. "You have almost none of it left," I continued. "I cannot let you waste it on me."

"It is my ointment," she replied, "and I'll waste it however I like." She helped me remove my armored jacket and the padded undershirt beneath it, then wiped both ends of the wound with the rag before applying the blue salve. I felt the pain leave my shoulder, and for a moment felt light headed.

"It's all gone," I said, as she rubbed in the salve. "Everything I had, my good armor, my bow, my riding boots, my extra daggers... but the worst part is that I lost the magic bag."

"Magic bag?"

"It was dwarven made, from spider silk. I could put ten suits of armor in it, and it would only just be full and weigh no more than one suit."

"It had the enchantment of holding," she said. "It's too bad that you lost your things, but at least you kept your life." I nodded ruefully, and she put the lid on the empty jar. "There, that looks better." I saw that the wound had closed and was more than half healed; I moved it, and noticed only a dull ache. "I'm sorry I ran out of ointment before you ran out of injury."

"It is enough," I said. "I should not ask you for anything more, but I must. I need a place to stay."

She looked at me strangely. "You are welcome here, swordsman, as long as you need."

"You are too kind," I replied.

"We are comrades now, are we not?" she said, making an expansive gesture. "My house is your house."

"Comrades, aye," I said, putting my undershirt back on. "We still have a problem we must discuss," I said. "Pentalion. I had thought to be ambushed by some strange monster, or attacked by some subtle magic. The last thing I expected was that he would alert the watch and accuse me of murder and thievery."

"Indeed," she said. "And he lied, to boot, for you stole nothing from him."

"Only a young girl he was about to feed to a monster," I replied. "But I assume he claimed something different before the watch."

"He is powerful in more ways than magic. We'll need help to defeat him. Tell me, swordsman, have you any of the treasure you brought to Slateholm left?"

"Fewer than fifty crowns," I replied. "And a small handful of jewels of somewhat greater value."

"Good," she replied. "We will lie low for a few hours, then slip out and visit a nearby tavern."

"This is a strange time to celebrate," I replied.

"It's no ordinary tavern. We're going to a place called the Fox and Wolf, the meeting place of the Grey League. I'll introduce you as a member of a distant thieves' guild, perhaps the Fallen Knights of Ravenstone... that's far enough away that you'll likely not be found out. You'll have to pay tribute, but if you say you're on the run from the watch, you may only pay ten or twenty crowns."

"Why should I pay half my remaining treasure to thieves?"

"They're powerful," she replied, "and can help us avoid arrest. Also, the meeting hall is warded against magical eavesdropping. This place, I'm sorry to say, is not. It would be safer for us to discuss our plans there than here."

"Well enough," I said. "So I must pretend to be a thief."

"The leather armor you're wearing will serve nicely as a disguise. But you'll have to leave your sword here."

Those words put ice in the pit of my stomach. I could see in her eyes that she knew it, but she just smiled at me. John Northcrosse, who slept with his sword, would have to venture into a den of thieves armed only with a dirk... it was almost too much to contemplate.

Chapter 4: The Fox and Wolf

It was past noontime when we entered the Fox and Wolf. It looked no different than any other tavern in the Poor Quarter, small, poorly lit, and occupied by unsmiling men. Eldritch walked up to the bartender, and I trailed behind her.

"Two beers," she said without preamble.

The bartender found two mugs, wiped them with a rag and filled them. "Two silver," he said, and I drew a crown from my pouch and slid it across the bar. He took the coin without looking at me and said to Eldritch, "Who's your friend?"

"This is John. He's a Fallen Knight, and an old acquaintance, and the watch has taken an interest in him. In us both, I suspect."

"Yeah, heard," he said. I noticed he made no move to give me the change from my coin, but I held my silence. "G'wan back." Eldritch nodded, then picked up her beer and walked toward the back of the room. I took mine and followed.

She passed through a narrow doorway into a corridor beyond; it ran perhaps fifteen feet, with a door on each side and one at the end, the latter having a peephole in it. Before she reached the door, the peephole opened, and a man's voice asked, "Who comes?"

"Eldritch of the Grey League and John the Fallen Knight."

"'E's a Fallen Knight, eh?" said the voice. "Yer both on the run then."

"Yes," she replied. "I claim sanctuary."

"That's well enough for you, but I don't know this John."

"I speak for him," she said, "and he brings twenty crowns, all he can spare, as tribute."

"Lemme see," he replied, and the peephole closed.

"We're not getting in, are we?" I whispered.

"Peace, John," she replied quietly. "He must ask the Guildmaster's leave for you to enter."

Shortly the door opened, and a short, portly, balding man was revealed. "Twenty crowns tribute, and yer in." I counted out the twenty crowns and he let us pass.

The room beyond was just as dimly lit, but much larger than the front room of the tavern, and it was filled with round tables spaced well apart from each other. A few tables were empty, but most had one or two people at them. The table in the far back of the room had three men and a woman sitting at it, with two chairs remaining.

Eldritch started toward one of the empty tables, but one of the men at the far table raised his hand and made a gesture of invitation. "Damn," she whispered to me, "the Guildmaster wants to speak to us. Keep a cool head and a closed mouth and we'll get through this."

I followed Eldritch to the table. She bowed, and I did also, hoping I mimicked her properly. "Good day, Guildmaster," she said.

"Good day, Eldritch. Please sit. Your friend also."

So we were obliged to join them. The Guildmaster was as nondescript a man as I've ever met; I'd never have given him a second look, nor ever believed he was in charge of a criminal empire. The two other men sat to his right; one of them was younger, but bore a resemblance to the Guildmaster, and I took him for son or maybe nephew; the other man was between them in age, blessed with a ready smile. I didn't trust his eyes, though. The woman sat at the Guildmaster's left but her pose seemed to indicate that she was not "his" woman. She was beautiful, pale skin and dark hair done in an elaborate style, and a low-cut dress showing her ample assets. Up close, she appeared older than she had at a distance, with a few fine wrinkles that makeup didn't quite cover.

Eldritch took the left chair, leaving me the right, between her and the woman. I considered holding Eldritch's chair for her, but she pulled it out and sat quickly, as a man would, without waiting for any show of chivalry. So I did the same, and waited to see what would transpire.

"I understand you have gotten yourselves into some trouble," the Guildmaster said. "Pentalion has entered a warrant against you."

"Yes," said Eldritch. "The job went wrong, and we need to lay low for a while."

It was about then that I noticed the bowls and utensils before the four of them, and the smell of stew came to me, and my stomach growled. The woman suppressed a snicker, but did not interrupt.

"You made a try at the house of a wizard," he said, "with a thief who hadn't yet paid his respects to me. I've a mind to censure you, girl."

"My apologies," she said. "I was working alone, and so was he."

She gave me a gentle kick then, and I said, "I tender my apology also, Guildmaster. It was foolish of me."

"You've manners, at least," he said. "They say Pentalion's doors and windows are all warded with magic. How did you get in?" Eldritch started to answer, but he said, "No, let John tell the story."

"I used a potion, sir, which gave me the power to throw my voice. I knocked at the back door, staying out of view of the peephole; each time the guard within closed it again, I knocked again, until he became angry and opened the door. As soon as the door began to open, I threw my voice behind him and fooled him into turning away, and then I ended his life with my dirk."

I've always been a poor liar, but as my story was mostly true, I hoped it would pass. The Guildmaster looked at me a moment, then said, "Clever boy."

"Thank you, sir," I said.

"Was that the murder you stand accused you of?"

"Yes, sir. He wasn't even a man, but a hobgoblin. I didn't know that Eldritch had entered unseen behind me, but shortly we met. Renewed our acquaintance. We didn't get much further before we faced more hobgobins, and unfortunately Pentalion saw us before we could escape. Worse yet, we got nothing."

He looked at me a long time, then turned to my companion. "Eldritch, don't lie to an old liar. This John," he said, waving at me, "he's no thief."

"Sir, wait," she said, but he raised his hand and she fell silent. For a few moments more, no one spoke.

"You're right," I said, breaking the silence. "I'm a swordsman by trade, and a barbarian by heritage." Eldritch looked at me, alarmed, and I said to her, "There's no point denying it to this man. He's too smart for that."

He laughed then. "You know how to get on my good side, barbarian."

"John really is my name. John Northcrosse."

"Magnus Tullock," he replied, stretching out his hand. I stood up, so as to reach him across the table, and took it. "It is a pleasure to meet you." I sat back down, and just then a pretty young woman brought a bowl of stew for each of us. My stomach growled again, reminding me that I had not eaten since the night before. "Eat, barbarian, before your stomach drowns us out," continued the Guildmaster, and they all laughed at his jest. So I dug in with good appetite.

"Was this deception your idea, Eldritch?" he asked then.

Looking sheepish, she said, "Yes, sir."

"I heard a rumor that a half-elven woman was seen bringing a young girl in nightclothes home last night," he said. "Truth, Eldritch... you didn't go into Pentalion's tower to steal treasure, but to rescue the girl."

"Truth, Guildmaster," she replied, eyes downcast. Then she met his gaze and continued, "He had been taking girls for several nights, to feed to a monster in his dungeon."

The woman shivered. "I've always thought he had an unnatural interest in young girls."

"Doesn't matter. He's powerful," said the younger man. "Among the wizards he's considered a leader, and he has the ear of several in the Prince's court."

"He surely means to get revenge on you," said the Guildmaster.

"Indeed," I said. "We may need to strike first. He is a mad dog, and mad dogs must be..."

"Hold, barbarian," interrupted the Guildmaster. "It's not our business. In fact, it's bad business. I will permit you to visit us here, but I do not want to know of your plans."

"We understand," said Eldritch, her hand on my knee silencing me. "Thank you for your time and the use of your hall." I sat back, looking at the faces arrayed around the table, all unreadable. It was not the sort of company I usually kept.

I looked down, and saw that my bowl was empty, but Eldritch still had half of hers. So I said, "Are you going to finish that?" and the woman beside me laughed out loud.

A little later, Eldritch and I excused ourselves and found an empty table. The serving girl came around as we got settled and asked if we would like anything.

"I'll take a beer," I said. "Eldritch, what of you? I'll treat."

"Wine," she said, "something red and sweet."

I grinned at Eldritch after the serving girl was gone. "Well, we're in," I said.

"Yes," she replied. "So now we may make our plans."

We hatched a great many plans that afternoon, but we threw them all away. Pentalion, it seemed, was too strong for us to take in a frontal assault, and too clever to sneak up on again, for it was a sure bet that my stratagem would not work again.

After a while, I leaned back and stretched, and said, "We are friends now, are we not?"

She looked at me, unreadable, then said, "Yes, I suppose." She smiled grimly. "We might as well be friends, and die together, as enemies who die together."

"Come, it's not that bad," I said. "We will win out, I know it."

"Perhaps," she said. "Tell me about you, swordsman. Where are you from?"

"I am from the northlands, born in a village in the shadows of the Demonfrost Mountains. Why, where are you from?"

"Here," she said. "I've lived my entire life in Slateholm, or at least in sight of its walls."

"Indeed," I said. "Have you never wondered about the world beyond the city? It's why I left my village... I wanted to see it all."

"I've seen people from all over the world," she replied. "All types of people come here... men of Corvis and Ravenstone and the many smaller places, the elves of Avenrho, dwarves from the mountain kingdoms. Why go elsewhere when all come here?"

"Indeed," I said again. "Your reckoning is unassailable." I drained my beer, then said, "I wish I had not lost the bag. Though I feel its loss more than its contents, having my good metal armor would make me feel... less exposed. I can hardly afford to replace it now."

"Was the rest of your treasure in the bag, then?" she asked.

"No. What is in my pouch is all I have left. Though I did have things I could have sold or traded."

"You're surprisingly short on treasure, for one so recently returned from looting an ancient temple," she replied. "Will you tell me what became of it?"

"I was grieving the loss of my friends. For almost five years we had travelled together, facing men, beasts, and monsters together. They were my friends, and it was right that I honor them." I paused, draining my cup. "I got drunk on the wines of Avenrho in honor of the elf we called Toliver because none of us could manage his real name. I got drunk on stout dwarven ale in honor of Ularic, who often joked that I was too tall for my beard, and I replied he was too short for his. I got drunk on the port our wizard Argent favored. I had never really cared for him or for his wine, but he stood with me in our final battle in Nol after the rest lay dead, and I drank his wine to honor his bravery."

I paused a moment, taking hold of my grief, still fairly fresh and wickedly clawing at my soul. "Brother Radric the Reformer was of this city, so when I was again sobered I sought out his people and told them what had become of him. I drank tea with them in honor of his passing. That left only Belgarett, our thief, to honor."

"Belgarett?" she said. "I knew of him, I think... a man of Corvis, slight of build with squinty eyes? He was of the guild of the Black Glove, but when he visited

Slateholm he paid tribute to the Grey League, and I saw him here once."

"If you knew him, then you knew that his vice was not wine, nor women either, though he enjoyed both."

"No," she said, "he was a gambler."

"He sought out the best gambling houses in every city we ever visited, and he spoke incessantly of them. So I visited his favorite house in this city and I gambled in his honor. For a while I was winning, which I took as a sign of his favor, but eventually I fell behind. At least I left before I could become indebted."

"So you honored your dead in their own ways," she said, bowing her head as if in thought. "It seems fitting."

"When I had seen to all of that, I was left without purpose. I considered joining a merchant's caravan as a guard, or seeking such duties in the house of some noble or wizard. I even considered joining the watch, if you can believe it." She laughed gently. "Then I heard that young girls were being taken from their very beds in the night, throughout the Poor Quarter, and my curiosity got the better of me. I soon deduced that Pentalion was the guilty party, and you know the rest."

"Yes. You became a hero, and a wanted man."

"Just so," I replied. "Tell me, sorceress, what purpose the young virgins served. I have heard of rituals that require the blood of a virgin to summon the lower powers."

"This is not such a ritual," she replied. "Though I could well believe that monster came from some other world, Pentalion had been taking girls for many weeks. I believe sacrificing young virgins was not the will of the monster in the pit, but of the monster in the wizard's soul."

"I suspected as much," I replied grimly. "Such a man does not deserve the privilege of continuing to breathe."

"I agree," she said. "We should go. I cannot just sit here all day long. Let me show you around the Poor Quarter."

"Is that safe?" I asked. "I feared every moment of our trip here that the watch would suddenly appear and surround us."

She grinned at me then. "The watch patrols the Poor Quarter scantily if at all. It is sometimes a dangerous place for the watch, so they come only in large groups."

"Well then," I said, "by all means, sorceress, be my guide."

Chapter 5: The Wizard Strikes

We spent the latter part of the afternoon into the evening walking the streets of the Poor Quarter, and I learned something important about Eldritch... she knew everyone, or at least it seemed so. She called everyone by name, shopkeepers and beggars and prostitutes and all the others she met, and they all seemed happy to see her.

At dusk, we were on a street a few blocks from the abandoned temple when I saw a pair of men in the robes of Reformer priests a block or so away. Eldritch hissed quietly, then took me by the arm and guided me to the other side of the street so we would not pass close to them. I tried to ask her why, but she would not speak of it. "Later, swordsman" was all she would say.

As soon as Eldritch judged it dark enough, we returned to her hideaway. We had bread and cheese and salted meat bought at stands in the marketplace for our supper, and I had purchased a skin of sweet red wine for us to share. She sat in the chair, and I sat on the rugs, and we drank our wine from mismatched cups meant for tea, and it was good.

"Tell me, sorceress," I said, "why we avoided those Reformers on the street today." She looked at me for a moment, irritation in her eyes, and I wondered what I'd said wrong. "You did say 'later,' didn't you?"

"Much later," she replied. "You needn't ask again."

"I'm sorry, Eldritch," I said. "I do not mean to pry."

Her face softened then. "I know, swordsman." She took a sip of her wine, then said, "Recall I said that only large parties of watchmen come to the Poor Quarter?"

"I do."

She smiled mischievously. "Such a party was there this afternoon, looking for us."

"What!" I exclaimed. "And there we were, wandering about like lambs to the slaughter!"

"Not so," she replied. "I knew where they were the whole time."

"By magic?"

She laughed. "No. We of the Grey League have our ways. We are the guild of thieves, are we not?"

"Indeed," I replied. Sensing there was more, I leaned forward, my food forgotten.

"We are also the guild of beggars, and of prostitutes. As we wandered the Quarter, I knew by the words and signs of those members of the guild who were about where the watchmen were. Once they were only a street away from us, yet we were never in danger of being discovered." She sat back then and drank deeply of her wine, wearing an expression most smug.

"Clever," I said in response. "Your organization is a marvel. I've seen crack military units who could not do so well."

"I thought you were freelance," she said. "When did you serve?"

"I never served as a soldier," I replied, "but on several occasions my friends and I helped defend one border fort or another." Our conversation lapsed for a time as we ate together in companionable silence.

When the food and the wine were gone, Eldritch said, "In the morning we must find a way to attend to our situation." She stood up and stretched, catlike, and against my better judgement I admired her lithe yet curvaceous figure. "Now I would sleep." With that, she retired beyond the hangings, and she covered the glowing doorknob as she had the night before.

I rolled up my cloak for a pillow, said "Good night" and laid down under the borrowed blanket with my sword. Eldritch replied in kind, and in moments I was asleep.

I was on my feet, sword in hand, before I was fully awake. It was nearly pitch dark. Some loud noise had awakened me, but before I could remember what it was, I heard it again... a loud pounding at the trap door. It was held with a heavy iron bolt, and I thought surely no one could break it open by main force.

Everything happened at once... I turned to face the trap door, the room was suddenly brightly illuminated, and the trap door flew open with a rending crash. I raised my right hand to shade my eyes, trying to see who or what was coming through the trap door, but I saw nothing.

The next thing I knew, I was lying on the floor with the wind knocked out of me. It had felt like being punched in the gut by an ogre, an experience I remembered well, but there was no ogre in the room. As far as I could see, I was alone on my side of the hangings.

I got to my feet as quickly as I could, holding my sword in front of me, even as Eldritch looked out through a gap in the partition. "It's something invisible," I said, waving my sword left and right and backing up to the curved wall.

Even as I said it, I saw the hangings move as if struck, and her face disappeared suddenly. I heard the *thump* of her body falling to the floor on the other side.

I would have no help from that quarter, it seemed, so I began to move around the area, sword waving, trying to find our invisible assailant. I listened for his footsteps as I moved, but I heard none, not even the creaking sounds I had already grown accustomed to in the attic. Almost too late I realized my opponent might be flying... I felt the wind of its passing as I ducked and swung wildly overhead. Though I expected nothing, I felt my sword strike a glancing blow to my invisible opponent, but it made no sound of pain or anger. I wondered, despairingly, if I had hurt it at all.

I had backed around "my" side of the attic, and was now near the open trap door. I knew my opponent might try to knock me into it, so I tried to act as if I hadn't realized my danger. I was still waving my sword about in the air in front and above me rather aimlessly when I saw the hangings suddenly waver as if affected by a breeze... a breeze that was coming at me. At the last moment, I stopped pretending I didn't know where it was and chopped down with my sword in both hands fiercely.

I wanted to cheer when I felt my sword cut into the monster, for by now I had given up any hope that I faced a man. The enchanted blackened steel of my sword bit deep, but still it made no sound, and in its mad rush forward it bore me hard into the curving outer wall. I was dazed as I felt it pulling away from my sword, but I managed to hold on to my weapon. I rose to my feet as soon as I could and resumed my defensive stance.

Now the monster became more canny, rushing at me then pulling away, testing me to see how well I could find it. Soon it began landing glancing blows on my body while I failed repeatedly to hit it. At last I saw signs of its passage along the hangings again, and again I aimed an overhead chop at it.

It had fooled me this time; as I chopped, it veered off somehow and tripped me, and I fell into the hangings. My sword went across the cord that held up the hangings and I bore the entire mess of cordage and fabric down with me to the floor.

I saw Eldritch then, sprawled unmoving across a narrow bed where she had landed. I had no time to check her condition or indulge any curiosity about her private "room;" in fact, I had barely managed to stand up when the monster struck again, bruising my ribs and throwing me across the bed beside Eldritch. The bed, made for a much smaller and lighter occupant, collapsed under the strain of the impact.

Though slowed by the battering my body had taken, I dragged myself upright and brandished my sword. For a few moments, nothing happened... I was not attacked, nor did my wavering sword find the monster's body.

It was then that I saw it... the monster's shadow. It wasn't dark like the shadow of a mortal, but rather shimmering like the reflection of the sun from the waves of a pond. There was only one source of light in the room, and I decided that, assuming the monster's shadow was cast in the same way mine was, that the creature must be between the shadow and the glowing doorknob.

I tried not to smile as I walked forward slowly, pretending I didn't know where the monster was, waving my sword around at random. What I was really doing, naturally, was approaching my foe so as to strike, and when I judged I was close enough, I turned suddenly and attacked.

My first strike was a hit, and a solid one. I think the monster had let down its guard, thinking it had the better of me. It fled now before my onslaught, but I pursued it and slashed it again. It made a break for the trapdoor, but I was closer and threw it closed, and as the monster crashed into it I reversed my sword and stabbed downward with both hands, driving my sword through the monster's body and into the trap door.

My sword shook in my hands for a few moments, and then was still. I stepped back then, leaving it standing upright.

"You've killed it," said Eldritch. I glanced back and saw her sitting up in the ruin of her bed.

"I think so," I replied. "Are you alright?"

"I am," she replied, standing up and resettling her clothing. "I have a bruises and a sore head, but I'll be fine. You?"

"Much the same, save for the sore head." I stepped forward and knelt by the trapdoor, feeling for the monster's body, but I found nothing.

"It was one of the Unseen, a demon of air. They are faultless stalkers of prey, and being made of air, they simply disappear completely when killed."

"Pentalion's work."

"Aye," she replied. "Was this more what you were expecting, then? Attacked by a monster summoned by a spell?"

"Aye," I said, a rueful smile on my face. "I'll learn someday not to voice such thoughts."

"I doubt it," she replied, a smile in her voice. I freed my sword and put it away, then turned to look at her. She was regarding her wrecked bed.

"I was too much for it, I'm afraid," I said, then immediately worried that she would take my words wrongly.

"It was no fault of yours." She pulled the thin mattress from the bed and laid it out on the floor. "This will do until it can be repaired."

"We should check the doors below," I said. "It came in from there."

"Aye, it surely left one open." I opened the trapdoor and was about to descend, but she said, "No, swordsman, let me. If a door or window is open, your light might be seen by someone."

"I don't like it," I replied. "Call for me immediately if you encounter trouble."

"I'll whistle," she replied, and she descended into the darkness.

Left with nothing to do, I set about trying to restore the hanging partition to its place. My sword had cut cleanly through the cord, but fortunately it appeared there was excess at one end where it was wrapped around a cleat. I loosed it, tied the cut ends together, and then reanchored the loose end.

In the course of the battle, several items had been knocked about the room, and I picked up those that were on "my" side of the partition. I had made a point not to pay too much attention to the things on the other side; Eldritch had not wanted me to see them, so I did not try, though I was mighty curious. Naturally I had noticed the bed, as well as the fireplace and water barrel she had mentioned, but as to the smaller items, I had done my best to ignore them.

The items scattered on my side of the hangings were mostly things I had already seen, such as one of the cups we had used with the wine earlier. The other things were mundane, a hairbrush, a metal hand mirror, a few scattered papers which meant nothing to an unlettered barbarian. I piled those items I didn't know the place of on the chair for Eldritch to tend to when she returned.

On the floor near the trapdoor I found one thing that caught my attention. It was a doll, made of old and threadbare white fabric, stuffed with something lumpy. It was in the rough shape of a man, with eyes and mouth embroidered on the face, and a jacket made from a scrap of blue material. A tarnished silver coat-button embossed with a symbol of a pegasus on a shield was affixed to its jacket.

As I was regarding it, Eldritch returned, saying, "It came in through the front doors. I've secured them again, but we'll need nails to..." It was then that she saw the doll in my hand, and she snatched it from me, a look somewhere between panic and anger on her face.

"I'm sorry," I said. "It was on the floor just here. We need never speak of it, I promise."

Rather than answer me, she disappeared through the hangings. I considered lying back down to sleep, but as she had not covered the doorknob I thought waiting a while the best course.

I waited quite a while, and was just reconsidering that decision when she appeared suddenly from behind the hangings again. "I'm sorry, John," she said simply, arms folded. "You did not know."

"I accept your apology, Eldritch," I replied, "and I say again that we need never speak of it." She nodded once, a look I took for relief on her face. "We should sleep, if we can. Perhaps we should stand watches so that we're not surprised again."

"A sound plan," she replied, suddenly businesslike. "You sleep first, swordsman." I began to protest, but she said firmly, "It makes more sense. I can see in the darkness, and I believe I'm less injured than you. If you are needed, I will wake you." Then she covered the doorknob. I laid myself down beside my sword under the borrowed blanket and fell asleep in the darkness, under the watchful eyes of Eldritch, and felt safer than I had in some time.

Chapter 6: Unexpected Visitors

I awakened to sudden illumination. "My turn, swordsman," said a woman's voice, and for a moment I wasn't sure where I was, but then I remembered. Eldritch.

"Good morrow, sorceress," I replied, sitting up. She was standing near the hangings, where I assumed she had just uncovered the glowing doorknob. "May I have a moment's privacy?" I said, nodding toward the chamberpot-cabinet.

"Of course," she said. "I'll go down and check the doors, and bring up a bucket of water from the cellar. If that will be long enough?"

"I expect so," I said. I was, in fact, done by the time she returned, and had quenched my thirst and thrown a bit of water on my face as well.

Upon her return, I said, "Any signs of trouble in the night?"

"None," she replied. "Summoning the Unseen is hard work, so I'm not surprised we only faced one."

"We must take action. Thus far, since our foray into his tower, the wizard has been on the offensive. We must bring the battle to him."

"I agree," she said, "and I have some thoughts on that... wait." A concerned look came into her eyes, and then she said, "We're being watched."

"Good morrow," said male voice softly from behind me.

In a single move I drew my sword, whipped around to my left and aimed my mightiest backhand swing at the space from which the voice had issued. As I turned I saw the smiling face of the portly wizard Pentalion, and my sword cleaved into his left shoulder.

And passed right through. My swing was on a downward arc, and the sword passed without resistance from his left shoulder to his right hip, thence onward to the floor where the blade hit with a *thunk* and became momentarily stuck. Worse, my wild swing had thrown me off balance, and I stumbled sideways, colliding heavily with the wall. Altogether not my best showing.

"Really, Eldritch, what are you doing with him?" said the illusion of Pentalion. "Clumsy oaf, whose only means of interaction with the world is by way of his sword. What can a clever sorceress like yourself find interesting in him?" He gave me an appraising look. "Or is he good in bed?

She replied, "He is more than you give him credit for, Pentalion. As am I."

"Please," he said, his emphasis indicating disbelief. "I shouldn't be surprised you chose to consort with him, indeed to ally with him against me. You are a journeyman magic-worker... you've mastered the spells of flying and of countering magic, neither of which are easy. Yet for all your talents, when your mistress was slain you reverted to type. Just a street waif, a thief, using the amazing gift she gave you for the pettiest of purposes."

"I have helped many," she replied, indignant. By that time I had regained my balance and assumed a defensive posture, though I was unsure what good that would do against an illusion.

"Poor people. Beggars. The lowest of the commoners... they should be bowing at your feet," he continued. "You could be wealthy, or at least well off, but what do you do?" He waved his hand around, indicating the attic I assumed. "You squat here, in an abandoned tower, rather than living in the sort of fine house a practitioner of the arcane arts deserves." He laughed then, a laugh that sounded strangely distant.

"What are you here for, wizard?" I yelled, my temper failing at last. "What do you want of us?"

"Why, to make you an offer," he said, his hands open before him. "You vexed me, and you continue to vex me. By slaying the hydramander, you set my research back perhaps a year... revenge would be sweet, but I have more important things to do. So, I'll make a deal with you. Leave Slateholm, and I will forget I ever met you. You won't have to look over your shoulders constantly, nor sleep in shifts. At least, not on my account. What say you?"

There was no moment when I found that offer tempting. Even had I believed he would honor an agreement, which I did not, I could not have lived with myself knowing I had a man such as him in reach of my sword and did not slay him. I glanced at Eldritch and saw my feelings mirrored in her eyes.

Before either of us could answer, he said, "I see you are considering turning down my generous offer. Before you do so, recall that besides being a powerful wizard, I am a respected citizen of the first water, with friends in the house of the Prince himself. You are a known thief and part-time sorceress and a foreign barbarian. What chance do you have?"

Eldritch raised her hand and said, "*Interecti,*" and Pentalion disappeared as though he had never been there. "That was quite enough of him."

"How did he appear, sorceress?" I asked. "And can he use that magic to find us?"

"I had heard that he owned a scrying mirror, by which means he could spy upon any person he knew. Such things do not reveal the location or even direction of the target creature, so fear not on that account."

"And he could send that illusion in the same way?"

"Just so," she replied. "As I understand it, his options for offensive magic are very limited, else I would have counterspelled him immediately." She frowned. "So why did he bother to contact us? Did he think we would accept his offer?"

"I wouldn't trust him," I replied.

"Nor would I, and he knows it. There must be some other reason..."

Just then, distantly, I heard a familiar sound... a huntsman's horn. Then again I heard it, closer, and looking around me I realized what he had done.

"Sorceress, I fear he may have learned our location," I said. "This building is distinctive, is it not? I have seen few of these onion-shaped domes in the city."

Her mouth fell open then, and her eyes went wide. "You are right. Curse me for a novice, he would know that this is the only one in the Poor Quarter. Come, we should flee if we still can." With that, she threw on her cloak and moved immediately to the trapdoor. I put my sword back in its scabbard and drew my dirk instead, in case we might have to fight in close quarters, and I followed her.

"Did you hear the huntsman's horn?" I asked, as she began to descend.

"I did," she said, "but I didn't recognize the sound. Such things are rarely heard in the city."

"We are the prey," I replied.

"Indeed." At the landing, she opened the interior door, which I had not yet passed through. Beyond it the temple formed a single large room, rounded at the near end and squared at the other. Tall, mostly broken glass windows lined the side walls and flanked the large double doors at the far end, but little light came in as they were boarded over on the outside. The sanctuary into which we had entered lacked the altar I had expected, but was separated from the main body of the temple by a low railing with an open gate in the center. Above the double doors were two small windows that were not boarded and thus admitted just enough light to move around by.

On another occasion, I would have been worried about offending the god to whom the place was still surely consecrated, but it didn't seem important at that moment. We were hunted, and I felt it as surely as if the huntsman's dogs were breathing down my neck at that very moment.

I followed Eldritch to the large doors, and saw the damage wrought by the Unseen the night before; the bar lay splintered on the floor some distance from the doors, and the cast iron brackets meant to hold it were shattered. My companion had secured the doors the night before by means of iron spikes driven between door and threshold, and inspecting her work I saw that nothing more could be done to secure them. The spikes would not hold against a determined effort to open the doors, particularly if those seeking entrance used a ram.

"Come here," she said quietly. Eldritch was standing on tiptoe, looking through one of the broken windows, and I saw the boards outside had a large enough gap to act as a peephole. I had to bend slightly to look through the crack.

Outside I saw two men in chainmail armor; their surcoats were not the green, silver, and black of Slateholm but rather red trimmed in gold, with a symbol of an inverted five-pointed star in a circle embroidered with black thread upon the chest. Both had huntsman's horns slung over their shoulders. "Pentalion's livery," she whispered in my ear, but I already suspected that.

"I thought he had only hobgoblins," I whispered back.

"It seems he has hired someone new." Even as she said this, I saw another man trot up, similarly dressed and equipped, and one of the two standing there immediately directed him toward the alley beside our hideout.

"That makes at least three," I said, and as I said it another arrived. "Four now. They must have spread out over the quarter looking for some sign, and the one who saw the sign blew his horn to gather the others."

"Then every moment we stay here, swordsman, the odds against us increase," she said. "We should escape now."

"How?" I said, turning to face her. "Have you some magic you haven't revealed to me? If we go out among them now, we might kill a few, but if there are very many still to come they will pull us down before we can win through."

She was about to reply, but was interrupted by a loud voice from outside. "John Northcrosse! I know you're in there!"

Putting my eye to the slit, I saw a large man in plate and mail, with a round steel shield and a longsword in hand. He too wore the surcoat of Pentalion, but his better equipment indicated he was of higher rank than the others.

"I know you're in there," he repeated. "I am Grantier, captain of this company. As you can see, Pentalion has upgraded his security force... no more does he depend on hobgoblins to do a man's job." He paused a moment, then continued. "You are surrounded. While our master distracted you, we waited for his sign, and even now I can see his blood red raven on the peak of the roof. If you come out peacefully, I promise to see to it that your death is quick, and that of your pretty companion too."

"Grantier!" I said, forgetting to whisper, though I saw no sign that anyone outside heard me. Eldritch looked at me, puzzled, and remembering to whisper I said, "He is reputed to be among the greatest swordsmen in the world, skilled, strong, fast, and crafty, and his company among the best trained. Pentalion paid a pretty penny for their services."

"Can you defeat him?" she replied.

"Maybe," I said, not entirely sure I was telling the truth, "but I cannot defeat his whole company, not even with your help."

"Then we flee," she said, grabbing my right hand and dragging me toward the rear exit. Even as we exited the sanctuary, I heard the thunderous sound of a ram striking the front doors. Eldritch turned down the cellar stairs, and I followed, hearing as I did the sound of men hammering and prying at the back door, mere feet away from me.

On the unlit staircase I was obliged to use my coin for light to see by, lest I trip and fall, bearing Eldritch with me down the stairs. The staircase curved down to the right into darkness, and opened up into a circular room, slightly smaller than the attic space we had just vacated. Chunks of masonry and other debris were scattered on the floor around a well situated in the center of the room. "Is there some secret door here, then?" I asked, looking around.

"No," she said. Stepping up to the well, she said, "We're going down here."

"How?" I said. "You might be able to climb the sheer wall down, but I cannot, and we brought no rope with us." I had noticed that the well seemed to have no rope, and in fact the stanchions provided to hold a winch were empty.

"Magic," she said. "I will fly us both down."

"You jest," I replied. "I have great respect for you, but you cannot be strong enough to carry me."

"I'm not," she said, "but I have no time to instruct you in using the magic the spell provides, so this is the only way. Trust me." She stepped up onto the rim of the well, said, "*lafflictis*," and stepped off into space. "Come here," she said, levitating above the center of the well.

I heard a splintering crash upstairs, and knew they had a door open, though I knew not which one. Having no time to discuss further, I stepped up on the side of the well as she had, my head brushing the low ceiling. She said, "Put your arms around me and step off," and I did.

When I stepped off, we began to descend. We were going down faster than I would have liked... the sides of the well, illuminated crazily because our only light was pressed between us, seemed to speed by, and I was sure we would lie broken side by side at the bottom of the well in another moment.

We landed with a splash in waist-deep cold water. I breathed a sigh of relief, and then the lights went out completely.

I must have made some sound, because Eldritch whispered in my ear, "Be silent, and follow me." I reached for her hand, but then I felt a tug at my neck, and I realized why the light had gone out... she had my coin entirely enclosed in her gloved hand, and was leading me by the thong I wore it on.

So naturally I followed her... what else could I do? I surmised we were not merely in a well, but actually following some underground stream. She led me downstream, and after some distance she whispered, "Duck your head."

Glad this time to have the guidance, I did so, raising an arm to help me gauge the height of the ceiling. Finally she stopped me, and released my coin so that I could again see. We seemed to be at a dead end.

"Beyond here we will have to swim underwater, or at least crawl along the bottom. I promise there is air beyond, and if you keep your wits about you, you'll get to breathe it."

I felt a little stung by that comment, and I said simply, "Lead, sorceress, and I will follow." She turned, drew a deep breath and ducked beneath the water, and I did the same.

The passage seemed to take forever. In the cold water my hands swiftly became numb, making it hard to be sure if I was making progress. My lungs were burning, and it was all I could do to resist the urge to inhale. Though I trusted Eldritch's word, still I began to despair of ever making it through...

Chapter 7: In The Tunnels

I bumped into something, and for a panicked moment thought I had become lost, but my cold hand managed to identify it as Eldritch's boot planted on the stream bottom before me. I turned myself upright as quickly as I could, and felt her hands lifting me under my arms.

As soon as my head broke the surface, I drew a long breath of air which, though stale and musty, was the sweetest I had ever known. I coughed a few times, then managed to climb over the stony ledge beside me. Eldritch, levitating, glided past me and I followed her.

The stony ledge proved to be the floor of a rectangular chamber with a low arched roof. One corner of the room had been eroded away by the action of the water beneath, and it was through that aperture we had arrived. At one end of the room I saw an open exit, with a staircase ascending beyond it, while at the other end was a wooden door bound with verdigrised brass bands. The room was entirely empty, the floor clear of debris of any sort, but I thought I saw here and there faded footprints such as those I was making with my wet boots.

"Where are we, Eldritch?" I asked.

"In the old tunnels," she replied, removing her cloak and rolling it, wringing out some of the water. "They say the tunnels under the Poor Quarter were once part of some older city, conquered by the ancestors of our Prince. It is said there are monsters down here."

"So have we left the proverbial frying pan for the fire?" I asked.

"Maybe," she said, shrugging. "But I doubt Pentalion's men will even know where we have gone. His mirror will likely not work for some time now, since I dispelled it, but even if he saw us here, how would he guess where here is?"

I looked at her, suspicious. "Do you know where here is?"

"Not really," she said, grinning. "This is as far as I've explored these tunnels. I have no idea what is beyond here." Then her expression changed suddenly, as I was learning it often did. "Now I too have lost almost everything to Pentalion, just as you did."

"I still live," I said, "and so do you. I have a good sword and a trusted companion. What more could I need?"

I could see this was little comfort to her, and though I was unsure if my attention was welcome, I put my arm around her shoulders. "I lost the doll," she said.

"All the rest, even my spellbook, I can replace, but it was all I had left of my mother."

She ducked her head, to hide a tear it seemed, but she had already failed at that. "We are friends, are we not?" she asked, and I nodded. "I barely remember my mother. I had seen five winters when she disappeared. I was taken in by a poor family who knew her, but my foster father was cruel, so when I was seven winters old, I ran away. I fell in with thieves, members of the Grey League, and I learned the art of stealing. They were more family to me than those I had run away from." She stopped a moment, wiping the tears from her eyes. "Never mind," she said, slipping out from under my arm. "Time enough later to mourn that silly doll."

I could think of nothing else to say, so I changed the subject. "We need to keep moving, sorceress. Wet as we are, we need to be warmed by exertion lest we chill, at least until we dry out. So perhaps we should explore." I looked at the staircase, and then at the brass-bound door. "Which way should we go?"

"The staircase ascends," she replied, "but for the moment, remaining underground seems our best choice."

"The doorway, then," I replied. Long experience had taught me not to touch anything in a dungeon without first examining it, and I spent a moment studying the door. Eldritch joined me, crouching to examine the door handle.

"I do not see a lock," she said, "and the handle is a simple pull, with no visible latch."

"It appears ordinary enough," I replied. "Shall I try it?" Rather than reply, she stood aside, one hand extended palm up toward the door. I took hold of the handle in my right hand, a habit I cultivated in case a trap should injure me; were I to suffer an injury to my good left hand I would be severely limited. But the door was stuck, much as I had expected, so I grasped the handle in both hands and pulled; still it remained stuck.

"Perhaps we'll need to take the stairs, then," said Eldritch. "Or I could use a spell, though I'd prefer not to expend the power just now as I might need it later."

I stepped back a moment, frowning. I was unwilling to be beaten by a door in front of my new ally. After a moment's rest, I rolled my shoulders to loosen them up and returned to the door one more time.

Bracing my boot against the wall beside the door handle, I took hold of it with both hands and pulled hard. I felt it move just a little, giving me cause to believe I might succeed, so I relaxed a moment and then pulled with all my might.

It came open with a mixed sound of grinding, squealing, and scraping. It dragged the floor, having become warped by years of neglect underground, but by main force I opened it until we could easily walk through.

Beyond it lay a corridor, no more than five feet wide. I faced Eldritch, smiling, and said, "After you?"

"Chivalry again," she said. "But then, I might be better qualified than you to scout ahead."

"No, sorceress, I was merely jesting. We go in together, shoulder to shoulder."

I drew my sword and took up a position on the right, so that my sword arm would not be against a wall. With Eldritch walking beside me we set out into the passageway.

"Pentalion spoke of your mistress," I said as we entered. "I never thought to wonder how you learned magic."

She laughed. "When I was young, I was cocky enough to try to steal from Melora, a sorceress, and was caught in a magical trap."

"How did you escape?"

"I didn't," she replied. "The sorceress told me that I had a heritage of magic, and gave me a choice... become her apprentice or she would turn me over to the watch. The punishment for thievery is the loss of a hand, so I chose instead to take her offer."

"Sensible girl," I said, nodding. We had gone down the corridor perhaps thirty yards then, whereupon we came to an intersection where a nearly identical passage crossed the one we were traveling. Eldritch indicated that we should proceed forward, so I did.

"I didn't really believe I could learn magic," she continued. "I stayed with her to buy time to plan my escape. She put a slave-collar on me, one with no keyhole; it was not magical, but without a keyhole, she said, how could I pick it? She told me when I knew enough magic to remove it, I was free to go."

"Thus she forced you to remain."

Eldritch laughed. "She thought so. It took me a month to discover a way to remove the collar without need of magic. I took it off and I fled through a window. I was free. I ran over the rooftops all night, pleased that I had outwitted the sorceress. But I had already learned a little, enough to realize that I could master magic if I tried. Before the sun rose, I was back in my bed in the tower of the sorceress, with the collar back on my neck, and I never told her I could remove it. Even after I did remove it by magic, I stayed with her."

Shortly we came to another opening, this one leading to the left into a large, low-ceilinged room, but again I proceeded forward at Eldritch's guidance. "So what happened to her, then?"

"As Pentalion said, Melora was slain in a duel with Tiberius Zara, the so-called Wizard of the West Wind. I never knew why she agreed to duel him. I always planned to seek him out and take revenge in her name, but he himself was slain in a duel with a wizard."

Just then another intersection became visible in my light. "The passage goes left and right, but does not continue," I said. "Which way now?"

She held a hand up, silencing me, and I saw that she was listening intently. "I think I heard something," she said. "Wait here, please. I will scout ahead; once away from your light, I will be able to see well enough in the darkness. I'll scout the way to the right first."

"I think we should remain together," I replied.

She smiled at me. "I'll be alright," she replied. "Wait for me." And with that she moved silently into the darkness, leaving me alone with my misgivings.

She had been away only a few moments when I heard a scraping sound, softly, from somewhere ahead. Listening, I heard it again, and then again, and I became certain I was hearing someone walking in the darkness, trying unsuccessfully to be stealthy. From that failure I felt sure it could not be Eldritch, for she had been entirely silent as she left. Realizing we were being stalked, I moved ahead slowly with my sword at the ready, drawing my dirk for good measure. Then I heard a feminine voice, her voice I was sure, cry out wordlessly a single time. I rushed forward toward the intersection.

Before I could reach it, a large figure stepped out from the left passage, and behind it another, and despite their pale white skin and pink eyes I recognized them as lizardmen. I had fought such many times before, and felt certain I could defeat two of them. They were armed only with spears, clad only in belts which supported simple loincloths, pouches, and scabbards holding daggers..

They stepped forward as I approached, and without words being said by either side, the battle was joined. The tunnel was too narrow for them to attempt to flank me, which was a mercy, but that very narrowness combined with the low ceiling hampered my swordplay without significantly affecting their spears. For a few moments I dodged and danced madly, deflecting their spears with my sword and my dirk while searching for an opening.

The lizard man on my right overextended himself in a strike which I deflected, and turning my dirk along the shaft of his spear I stabbed him in the gut. He fell, bleeding, and began to drag himself away from the fight. Now facing just one of the monsters, I felt sure I could prevail.

It was then that I was struck from behind, a harsh blow that brought the darkness down over my eyes and my mind.

I awakened in utter darkness, my head throbbing. I discovered myself disarmed and nearly naked, lying in foul-smelling straw. Unable to see, I began to feel around. Nearby was a wall, and after following it only a little way I found myself in a corner; as I turned to follow that wall, I heard a voice say, "How do you fare, stranger?"

The voice was masculine, a man no older than myself I judged, with the accent of a well-born native of Slateholm. "I have a sore head, but otherwise I'm in a fair state," I replied.

"I'm glad to hear it," he replied. "Though I'm afraid neither of us will stay in a fair state long." He paused, then said, "I'm sorry, been down here too long, forgot my manners. Hugh Hedgekin, second lieutenant of the watch."

A watchman! Custom demanded that I name myself, but I knew that if I told him my name, I might turn this potential ally against me. Still, knowing myself to be a terrible liar, I chose the truth. "I am John Northcrosse, adventurer, late of the Desert of Nol."

He replied, "It's a pleasure to meet you, though I'd prefer better circumstances." I counted as a blessing the fact that he showed no sign of knowing my name. "How came you here?"

"Struck over the back of the head as I explored a tunnel," I replied. Though honesty was my policy, I saw no reason to tell him more than was needful. "I had a companion, but we were separated. Have you had any sign of her capture?"

"I have not," he replied. "Exploring tunnels with a woman, eh? Hopefully she escaped our fate. I'm not sure how long I've been here, but I too had companions, and one by one they've been removed from this room and have not returned. I suspect the lizard men have eaten them, and they will soon eat us as well."

A chill ran down my spine and settled in my stomach, which inopportunely reminded me that I hadn't eaten since the day before. I continued to move around the room, stepping carefully and following the walls, until my toe bumped into something yielding. "Ouch, careful, man!" said Hugh's voice.

"My apologies," I said, reaching down and finding his bare shoulder. "You're quite cold."

"Truth," he said. "This dungeon is as chilly as it is dark."

"I suppose it is," I replied.

"How is it that you are not suffering from it?"

"I was born in the shadow of the Demonfrost Mountains."

"I see," he said. "So cold is like an old friend, then?"

"More an acquaintance than a friend," I laughed. "Well, best to finish familiarizing myself with the accommodations."

"The room is about fifteen feet square," he replied. "The door is just to the other side of me. It's quite solid, I'm afraid."

I carefully walked around his seated form and found the wall again, and then the door he had mentioned. It had no handle on our side, unsurprisingly. I hit it with my shoulder a couple of times, more to feel it out than to try to force it, and determined that it was indeed quite solid.

"We'll have to outsmart them," I said.

"How, when we can't even see them, while they apparently see us well enough?"

"I don't know. Let me consider a while." As I imagined and discarded one plan after another, I let my fingers tour the door, feeling its shape and size and looking for any flaw. I found none.

After a time, I gave up, and sitting down in the straw I engaged Hugh in conversation. Like Eldritch, it seemed he had spent his whole life in Slateholm. He spoke little of himself, but asked me incessant questions about my past until I found myself telling him my entire story, from the day I first left my home until I arrived at Slateholm. But I had presence of mind enough to end the story there, as I saw no point in alerting him to my present status.

Finally I said, "You asked me, but I never returned the favor. How came you here?"

"There were reports of ghosts in an area of the Poor Quarter; the area had long been thought haunted, and people would disappear from time to time, taken by the ghosts. The watch paid little heed to the reports, until they began to hear the same reports from a neighboring area of the Merchant's Quarter. Lieutenant Ancelin and I felt that they weren't ghosts, but rather some subterranean monster, so we got a squad together and went below to look."

I laughed ruefully. "It appears you were right."

"Yes. Too bad for the Ancelin and the others."

Just then, my stomach growled. "Do they ever feed us?"

"Nay," he replied. "I've been watered a few times, but have not eaten in what seems forever. Though in truth, I don't know how long I've been in here. Say, perhaps you can help me... my squad was taken on the eighth."

"I may have lost track, as I was not paying much attention to the calendar, but I believe it was the tenth or eleventh when we entered the tunnels."

"Well, that's longer than I wished, but less than I feared," he replied, yawning. Hearing his yawn, I was unable to resist yawning myself.

"Perhaps we should sleep, and conserve what resources we have." Hugh concurred, and I lay down in the straw and after some time I fell asleep to the sound of his snoring.

Chapter 8: Among The Lizard Men

I was on my feet before I was fully awake, clutching uselessly for my sword. It was still pitch dark... a noise had roused me, and I realized it was the door opening. I heard voices speaking a language of grunts and hisses, and then I was thrown hard against the wall, face first.

I knew immediately that they would bind my hands. It was not the first time a foe had bound me, and I had learned a few tricks in my adventuring career. I struggled, not enough for them to strike me, but just enough to conceal the fact that my arm muscles were fully clenched. This would make the bindings on my wrists looser, provided they didn't realize what I was doing. It was a trick Belgarett had taught me when we fought the slavers of Ravenstone.

To my great pleasure, the lizard man binding me did not seem to notice. The binding felt like heavy leather thongs, an inch or so wide, rather than rope.

As I was being half-led, half-dragged away, I said, "Hugh! Are they taking you too?"

"No, John," he replied. "It was a pleasure meeting you." Then I heard the door slam shut between us.

"And you!" I yelled back, and my captor cuffed the side of my head, grunting something at me. I didn't know his language, but his meaning was clear enough.

I was led for some distance down dark corridors, past several turnings; I could not see them, but I could hear the way the sounds changed as we passed various openings. I knew I was lost. Even if I had a light, I could not find my way back to the cell.

We turned once more, and I felt air movement for the first time. A definite draft was blowing down the new corridor, pushing us from behind. The air was not exactly warm, but it was less cool than in other parts of the dungeon complex, and better yet, it was fresh.

Ahead I noticed a glow, which resolved into an opening into a larger room. I smelled wood smoke before we reached the opening, and so was not surprised to see the large rectangular room had a stone-sided fire pit at its center.

The room was the largest I'd seen so far, perhaps forty feet long by twenty-five wide, and I judged it was nearly twenty feet to the arched ceiling. The entrance through which I was led lay near a corner along one of the longer walls; that entrance was an open archway, but directly across the room was a door secured with a heavy bar. I was puzzled for a moment by the draft entering the room, and the relatively smoke-free air within... where was the smoke from the fire going? Then I glanced up and saw a large opening in the wall high up on the short side nearest me, and realized it was acting as a sort of chimney.

Beneath that opening was a table which chilled my soul. It was a heavy table such as might be found in a kitchen in some high-born person's mansion. Though it had evidently been cleaned several times, the bloodstains on the table and on the floor surrounding it made it clear what its purpose was.

The wicked-looking knife lying upon it was clear enough warning by itself.

There were many lizard men in the room. I say lizard men, but I'll admit I cannot tell a male from a female; though females are said to be smaller, it's difficult to tell an adult female from a juvenile male. There were no very young juveniles present, only those old enough to take on adult duties. Every one of them wore a belt supporting a loincloth, pouch, and a dagger in a scabbard, but only a handful of the largest individuals carried spears.

I took in all that in just a moment, long experience in dangerous environments having taught me not just to look but to see. I now saw for the first time the three individuals who had escorted me from the cell. They guided me around the central fire pit toward the far end of the room. Unlike the rest of the dungeon, that room was not only warm but uncomfortably so. Being swamp dwellers, lizard men like warmth; I wondered at their choice to reside in the tunnels.

A wooden platform stretched across the back of the room, supporting a large chair that was being used as a throne by the largest lizard man I'd ever seen.

Lying on the floor to either side were four lizard women (for I was sure by their poses of submission that they were his females) while a total of seven large individuals armed with spears stood in a semicircle around the back of their leader. The lizard chief's right leg was twisted, as though broken and then badly set before healing, and he had numerous scars on his pasty white skin.

Then he spoke. "What is your name?"

"You speak Urdish," I replied, and at his nod one of my captors cuffed the back of my head. Smiling, I said, "I am John Northcrosse! I have fought men and monsters from the Demonfrost Mountains to the Desert of Nol. I have won a drinking contest with a dwarf, and a debate with an elf, and I have eaten the heart of a dragon. I do not fear you."

The lizard chief laughed briefly, sounding much like a large dog with a bad cough. At last he said, "Good, good. I like you. I look forward to hearing your screams when you are butchered." He stood then, and I saw for the first time that he wore my sword in its scabbard at his hip. He saw me looking, and he drew it. "Is big and sharp. Good sword." Then he put it away. "You came with elf woman, yes?"

"I don't know what you are talking about."

He nodded again, and again I received a blow to the head. "You lie, but I know better. We will find her. Elf has the best flavor." I couldn't resist then... even with my hands bound, I tried to rush him, but the lizard men at my sides stopped me.

He laughed again. "I like you," he said again, "so I save you for later." He then barked orders at my escort, and two of them led me toward the barred door. I wondered if they planned to put me in some new cell, but they stopped when I had a good view of the bloodstained table.

I saw two lizard men leave the way we had come, and for a while the inhabitants of the room ignored me. The lizard chief chatted quietly with his warriors, while absently petting the head of one or another of his females. One of the smaller lizard men, one I decided must be a female, walked to the table carrying two leather buckets which appeared empty. Placing them beside the table, she picked up the knife and felt the edge with her thumb.

I tried to ignore her. Looking around the room, I noticed some details I had ignored before, such as the formerly rich but now tattered wall-hangings behind the lizard chief's throne. The most interesting thing were the large urn-shaped covered baskets, almost as tall as Eldritch, arranged in a rough circle around the firepit. They seemed important, and I wondered what they held.

Soon the lizard men who had left returned dragging Hugh. His hands were not bound, but judging from his appearance he could not have put up much of a fight. Like me, he was nearly naked, having been allowed to retain only his breeches. His bruises made it clear he had been beaten, and that combined with lack of food had left him weak.

Without ceremony they threw him on his back on the table, and one of my remaining escorts went to help them hold him down as the female bound his hands and feet with thongs to the legs of the table. I now had only one escort, and rather than hold me, he simply held his spear horizontal in front of me.

Glancing around, I saw that the lizard men all appeared to be watching the activity at the table... even my escort. I took the opportunity to try my bonds... they were looser than the lizard man had intended, but were they loose enough for me to escape them? I worked at them as furiously as I could without attracting attention.

The female raised the knife, and I was sure I was too late... but she held that pose, as if waiting. I looked toward the platform, my struggle forgotten, and I saw an old, stooped lizard man I hadn't noticed before. He had to have been behind the row of warriors, I decided. He walked slowly from the platform, around the far side of the firepit, and up to the table. He was wearing several strings of small bones around his neck, fingerbones I thought, and as he raised his hands and began chanting I realized he must be a shaman.

He was blessing their meal. Hugh. Reminded of the urgency, I again began working at my bonds, twisting my wrists so that the leather cut into them, trying to stretch the leather enough to get my hands free.

The female turned to Hugh and reached out with the knife, apparently planning to gut him first. My hands were still trapped... there was nothing I could do as she lowered the blade. I was sweating, my heart pounding... I could not look away, though I did not wish to see a fellow man slain in such a way.

She cut the cord that fastened his breeches.

I was relieved, but only a little. It was only a matter of time before that knife was turned on his defenseless flesh, and I was still helpless to aid him.

Then I felt the leather begin to stretch... the sweat running from my body had soaked the thong, it seemed, and with that little bit of help I worked a hand free. The relief seemed to flow over me like a cool breeze.

I kept my hands hidden behind me as I worked the knot in the thong loose, for I had a use for it. I wrapped one end around my right hand and gripped it firmly. The female seemed to have stalled, having some difficulty in cutting the leg of Hugh's breeches; I wondered very briefly why they hadn't stripped him before binding him.

Even as I leaped at my remaining escort, I heard a shout arise from the platform, and he began turning to face me. I wrapped the thong around his neck and grabbed for it; catching the loose end on my first try, I pulled the thong tight while planting my knee in his lower back. He dropped his spear so he could try to get his hands under the thong, and that was the opening I was hoping for.

I snatched up his spear, swinging the butt end up into his snout. He fell as if poleaxed, and I turned the point of the spear toward the lizard men closest to me.

Most of the lizard men, including the chief and his seven largest warriors, were on the platform or near it; only three warriors, the priest, and the female with the knife were at my end of the room. The odds were not in my favor, but I saw that at least Hugh had not yet been harmed.

There was a moment when no one moved. Then it passed, and many things happened all at once.

I charged the nearest warrior, spear lowered, hoping to remove him from the fight before he could retaliate. He turned toward me even as I charged, trying to bring his spear to bear on me, but I was the barest bit faster. I plunged the spear into his gut and up through his heart, slaying him instantly, and he fell with the spear stuck in him.

Rather than let him bear me down, I released the spear. The nearest of the lizard people was now the female, and she was facing me with the knife held as an expert knife-fighter would; I did not dare bend down to pick up the slain warrior's spear. Worse, the remaining warriors were in ready positions, and out of the corner of my eye I saw all those at the platform were on their feet and moving forward, with their chief in the lead.

A feminine voice called out from somewhere behind me, "*Rappakora*." Instantly, a mass of webbing stretched between the walls at the far end of the room, trapping most of the lizard men, including their chief. Now the two warriors, the priest, and the female were the only lizard men free to do battle with me.

Without stopping to question the event, I feinted to the right, then swung my hardest left hook into the jaw of the female, and as she fell back she dropped the knife. The two warriors rushed me, and I did the only thing I could do... I ran around the table where Hugh was bound, forcing them to follow me. I was faster on my feet than they were, and by the time they figured out that they should circle the table in opposite directions, I had both the dropped knife and spear.

Holding the spear in my left hand and the knife in my right, I backed away from the table as the two warriors stalked toward me. I saw the priest then, cowering near the entrance, and was glad I didn't have him to worry about as well. I felt the heat of the firepit which I was backing toward and knew I was running out of room to maneuver.

I bumped into one of the tall baskets, and as it rocked back and forth the two warriors paused while the chief, trapped in the webbing behind me, began to scream orders at them. "What's in these baskets, then?" I asked, and not waiting for an answer I held the knife in my teeth and lifted one of the basket covers.

Inside was a large egg in a bed of straw. It was nearly as large as a man's head, white and slightly irregular, with a shell that looked leathery rather than hard. The chief's screamed orders became even more shrill, and the two warriors seemed not to know what to do.

Then one of the warriors facing me crumpled to the floor. Behind him I saw Eldritch holding a bloody dagger in each hand. Now the odds were even, and I closed with the remaining warrior before he could turn on her.

We battled for some moments, alternately stabbing and parrying each other. I had little experience using a spear, and was pleased to find I handled it pretty well; I was using it in both hands, with the knife still in my teeth. The lizard warrior was well aware of the danger of turning his back on Eldritch, so of course I repeatedly maneuvered to force him to do that. Each time he backed away rather than risk being flanked.

I was so focused on him that I never noticed the approach of the priest; the first indication I had of him was a cry of pain from Eldritch. I was distracted a moment, and the lizard warrior scored a hit to my left hip that might have been fatal had I not turned aside at the last moment. I continued my turn, smashing the butt end of my spear into the side of his head. He fell to the floor, apparently dazed but not unconscious, but that was the opening I needed to slay him with a thrust of my spear through his heart.

Eldritch was even at that moment striking a killing blow to the lizard priest. I dropped the knife into my hand and said, "Good to see you again, sorceress."

"Missed me, have you?" she said, smiling.

"Indeed. Eldritch, meet Hugh, second lieutenant of the watch," I said, pointing to the table. "You might free him if you're not too busy."

"And what will you be doing?" she asked as she moved toward him.

"I'll just be over here visiting with the chief," I replied. The lizard chief had been at the front of the group as they approached, and so was near the edge of the webbing. He had not drawn my sword; it hung still at his side.

"You should run," he said as I approached. I saw him struggling against the thick, sticky cords, and I could hear them beginning to tear from the strain. But I ignored his words and examined the webbing near his hip... it looked as if I could slip my arm between the strands and grasp the sword by the hilt.

Knowing I had little time, I decided to try my luck. I bent down and reached my right hand carefully into the mass of webbing, feeling the hairs of my arm catch on the sticky stuff and tear stingingly away. I touched the pommel, then slipped my hand down the hilt and grabbed it firmly.

The lizard chief chose that moment to struggle, pushing his hip to the side, and the sticky webbing was drawn across my arm. "Damn," I said, and he laughed.

"You are trapped, human. You will be here when we are free, and we will eat you yet."

I looked into his malevolent red eyes. "No, you won't," I said, and with that I pulled with all my might. I felt the cords begin to give way, but then my progress stopped, and he laughed again.

"Swordsman, you should have left it," said Eldritch. I looked and saw her trotting toward me; Hugh was standing beside the table, trying to keep his breeches up with one hand while holding a spear in the other. It looked as if it were the spear holding him up rather than the other way around.

"I will not," I said. "I've lost everything else. I won't lose my enchanted sword. Take my hand and pull." Eldritch took hold of my left hand and pulled, but still I couldn't pull free.

"Only one thing to do," she said at last. "Are you ready to run?"

"Yes," I replied.

The webbing suddenly disappeared. All of it. My sword came free of the scabbard, and without delay I turned and ran.

Hugh called, "This way!" and I ran toward the sound of his voice with Eldritch by my side. He had opened the barred door, I saw, and though I had no idea if he knew what he was about, I followed him through it.

To my surprise, beyond the door was a staircase leading up, lit dimly from somewhere above us. Not caring where it led, so long as it was away from the lizard men, I began to run up the stairs. Eldritch kept pace beside me easily, but we hadn't gone far before Hugh fell behind.

"Leave me," he said. I stopped when he did, and looking down the stairs I saw the lizard men charging, spears pointed up toward us.

Without a second thought I grabbed Hugh and threw him over my shoulder, then started up the stairs again. Eldritch was ahead of us, though I saw she had slowed a bit when we stopped.

The staircase seemed to go on forever, and the lizard men drew ever closer behind us; though Hugh's weight was slowing me, I would not abandon him no matter how much he insisted. Ahead I saw the light grow stronger, and realized it was leaking in around a door of some sort. Eldritch reached it first and began to struggle with the iron bolt that held it closed. It was stuck, I saw, and I did not know if we would get it open before the lizard men caught us.

At the last moment, Eldritch said, "*Fralineen*" and the door flew open. Without pause I ran blindly into the bright sunlight.

Chapter 9: We Escape

We were in a narrow alley in the Poor Quarter, judging from the appearance of the buildings around us. The door we had exited through was framed in the bright light of the setting sun, which by some fortune was lined up perfectly with the alley. Turning to face the lizard men, I realized they had stopped. I could just see them, standing low on the stairs in the shadows.

"They cannot bear the daylight," said Eldritch as I set Hugh back on his own feet. Then she came to me suddenly, smiling broadly, pulled me down and kissed me. I was stunned for a moment, then without thinking I began to respond to her kiss, but just as I did she broke it. She looked appalled at what she had done, and though I smiled at her she pushed away, crossing her arms.

Hugh cleared his throat, and said, "The sun will set in mere moments. We can't stop now." Looking around, he said, "This way." He pointed toward a crossing alley that branched north between two tall buildings, and we followed him around the corner. "I know this place," he continued. "Just yonder is the canal, and the Merchant's Quarter is across it. My parent's house isn't far."

"I do not care for the thought of walking the streets undressed as I am," I replied, following him into the alley.

"Then don't," replied Eldritch, and as I looked she turned and began to scale the wall of one of those tall buildings. They were tenements, I realized, cheap dwellings for the poor. Clotheslines were strung between the upper floors using pulleys, and as I watched Eldritch pulled down shirts and pants and threw them to us.

"I don't care for stealing," I complained.

"Fear not," replied Hugh, pulling on a shirt which very nearly fit him. "I'll come by here later and pay the occupants."

I quickly dressed, aware that the setting sun would free the lizard men to follow us. As soon as Hugh and I were covered and Eldritch had alighted, we set off toward the canal. Though our feet were bare, at least Hugh and I were covered as much as modesty required. I had slipped my sword into an extra pair of pants and rolled them up to conceal it. Carrying a naked sword around would have drawn too much attention, and of course I now had no scabbard for it.

The broad way beside the canal was full of people rushing to and fro, with merchants conducting their final business of the day while laborers hurried homeward, and though I felt all eyes were upon us, it appeared everyone took us for beggars. Eldritch walked a ways behind us, with her hood pulled low over her eyes.

We followed the canal for perhaps two hundred paces before turning up a broad street. "I'm not familiar with this area," I said to Hugh.

"Why, this is Broad Street," he replied, and at my laugh he looked puzzled, but I shook my head. Then he noticed a bill of some sort posted on a nearby building, and reached out to pull it down.

Looking over his shoulder, I saw it bore well-drawn likenesses of myself and Eldritch. Though I do not read, I do know my figures, and the amount quoted on the wanted poster read five hundred.

"So," he said, looking at me. "We'll talk of this later." With that he led us onward, folding the sheet and sticking it in his shirt.

The house to which he took us was large and well appointed. "We'll go around to the servant's entrance, if you don't mind," he said. "You'll draw less attention that way. My parents are visiting family in a village up the coast to the north, and my brother is at sea, but the servants will be home."

Hugh knocked at a back door, and shortly it was opened by a maidservant. "Master Hugh," she said in surprise. "What has become of you, sir? They said you were lost."

"Had a little trouble, that's all," he replied. "Let us in, girl, I'd rather not be seen this way." With that, she stepped back and he led us inside. Turning to me, he said, "My brother's clothes should fit you well enough, if you don't mind cast-offs." I shook my head, and he continued, "Let's get cleaned up and changed, and then we can have that discussion."

He led me to a guest room, and Eldritch waited outside the room as I washed up in water brought by the maidservant. By the time I was clean, he had returned, dressed in fine clothing, with an armload of clothes including a dark cloak and a pair of riding boots. The clothes and boots fit me tolerably well, and I felt human once more.

The three of us adjourned to the kitchen, where the cook provided us with leftover meat and bread and fried us eggs. Hugh and I ate with gusto, taking little time for discussion; in the presence of the cook and maidservant, he did not speak of the wanted poster, for which I was thankful. I marveled silently how we had gone from the squalor of that cell where we met to the luxury of his father's house in such a short time, and I thanked the gods for the blessing.

Later we went into a parlor and he closed the door. I settled into a comfortable chair, laying my sword beside me, while Eldritch took the chair furthest from me. Hugh placed three glasses of red wine on the low table in front of us, then took a seat himself.

He threw the wanted poster onto the table. "Tell me about this."

"We entered Pentalion's tower," I replied, "by cleverly fooling the not-so-clever hobgoblin guarding the back door. We believed he was responsible for the stories of poor children being stolen from their very beds in the middle of the night, and it turned out we were right. He was feeding them to a monstrous hydra in his dungeon."

"I see," he replied. "This poster says you are murderers. So who did you kill, then?"

"Hobgoblins," I replied. "Servants of the wizard."

"I did injure him," said Eldritch, practically the first words she'd said since the alley. "Or rather, caused him to be injured. He was flying above us, throwing lightning at John, and I countered his spell of flying."

"I heard his leg break," I added.

"Ah," he said. "That explains the charge of assault." He looked at me a moment, silent. "My duty is to bring you in, John Northcrosse. Both of you. But above my duty to the Prince lies my duty to the man and woman who saved my life... without you, I would surely rest in the stomachs of those lizard men."

"So we need not fight, then?" I asked.

"No," he replied, "and I'm thankful for it, for in my current state the two of you would surely lay me low. You may spend the night here. In the morning, I will return to the barracks and report all that has occurred. I will tell them that you fled after we escaped from the dungeon and I was unfit to follow you. Hells, it's at least half true."

"Thank you," said Eldritch, and I added my thanks.

"You needn't thank a man for performing his simple duty," he replied, taking a sip of the wine. I followed suit; it was less sweet than Eldritch preferred, but I rather liked it.

We talked of other subjects for a while. Hugh was very interested in the things we had learned of Pentalion, and though he didn't say I began to think that he didn't like the wizard any more than we did. But soon the combination of the wine and his exhaustion had the better of him, and he suggested we call it a day. "Will you be needing two guest rooms, or only one?" he asked, mischief in his eyes.

"Two," said Eldritch before I could answer. At his instructions the maidservant guided us to rooms across a corridor from each other, and left us to our own devices.

"Eldritch, wait," I said as she was about to close the door of her room. "I would speak with you."

"Later," she said, putting ice in her tone, but before the door closed I saw sadness in her eyes.

I was confused. As I set about making ready for bed, I wondered at her behavior. Her kiss had seemed genuine, and I had returned it, so I could not claim to her or to myself that I did not have feelings for her. I had been with women before, even thought myself in love once, but this time my feelings bore the stamp of authenticity. I was in love. I had to admit it.

But she had turned from me, shocked by her own action, and since then had been cold toward me. Why did she pull away? Was the kiss only a sign of friendship, as I knew was common among some peoples? Had my passionate response been improper?

It took me a long time to fall asleep, troubled as I was by the situation, but the wine and the food and the exhaustion of my struggles and injuries eventually took their toll on me, and I did sleep at last.

I awakened with a start. It was still dark outside, but there was a faint glow visible under the door of my room. I heard knocking, so I arose and went to the door. I had slept in my breeches; I considered getting dressed, but decided that anyone coming to my room in the middle of the night would have to accept me as I was.

I found Eldritch outside my room, fully dressed, with a candle in her hand. I said, "Are we leaving, then?"

"Not yet," she replied. "Please, John, can we speak? I know I treated you coldly, and I'm sorry."

"Come in," I said, stepping aside. The room had a magic lantern hanging from the ceiling, so I reached up and turned the key that opened its shutters, opening them just enough to light the room dimly.

"So tell me," I said, irritated, "why did you kiss me, then shun me? You play with my feelings. Am I just a toy to you? I thought we were friends."

"You don't understand, swordsman," she said, turning from me.

"Then explain it. You have my fullest attention."

She faced me again, arms crossed. "I cannot mate with a human," she said. "You have not considered what that would mean for me. Should I bear a child with a human, that child would be human too."

"I know this," I said. "Even children who know not of mating know this. Elf plus human is half-elf. Elf plus half-elf is half-elf. Half-elf plus human is human."

"You know it, but you have never thought about it," she said. "I might live more than two hundred years. If my child is human, she will wither and die before I am middle aged. It is a sad enough thing for a parent to outlive a child killed by disease or misadventure; to have your child die of old age while you are still hale and hearty would be unbearable."

"I see," I said. My heart was like a stone in my chest, but I strove to carry on. "So you must wed an elf or half-elf, then... but an elf would feel the same about marrying you as you would about marrying a human."

"Just so," she said, head bowed. "If I am ever to marry, it must be with a half-elf." She looked into my eyes then. "I do not dare even to dally with a human, for fear I will fall in love with him. I'm sorry, John Northcrosse, I cannot be with you." Tears began to run down her face then, and my stony heart broke from seeing them.

"Peace, sorceress," I said, putting my arms around her, though she kept hers crossed between us. "We are friends, and if that is all we may be, I will be content with it."

She looked up at me with tear-filled eyes. "Do you truly mean that?"

"I swear it," I said, though I knew not how I could. Compared to that task, my lonely and dangerous trek out of the Desert of Nol seemed little more than a stroll around town.

"Thank you," she said, embracing me at last. "It is good to have a friend." She held me for a moment, then broke away, her expression turned serious. "In an hour it will be morning; we should leave before then, to be fair to Hugh."

"I suppose," I replied, taking that as a hint to get dressed. "Where will we go?"

"I have an idea about that," she replied. "Last night while you slept, I searched the house."

"Eldritch!" I exclaimed. "Would you be so petty as to steal from our host?"

"Well, yes, but not the way you are thinking, John," she replied. "Hear me out, please."

"Very well," I replied. "Proceed."

"I was studying the exits, and considering the defensibility of the house should that become necessary. I paced off all the floors, looking for secret rooms, and I found one in the basement. Behind a secret door that I don't think had been opened in many years I found a shaft with a ladder going down."

"You want to go back into the tunnels, after our last experience there?" I asked, incredulous.

"Yes," she said. "It is too dangerous to walk abroad in daylight... I can hardly believe we passed through the Merchant's Quarter without watchmen pouncing on us. And John, when we went below before we were unprepared. This time we will have food and water, and I suggest we borrow the magic lanterns from our rooms."

"Borrow," I replied. "As long as we intend to return them."

"Hugh wouldn't mind. Recall his answer when I got you both clothing."

"Indeed," I said, sitting down on the bed to pull on the boots he had given me. "Still, I do not feel right taking from his family like this."

"If you asked, he would give them to you, I know it," she replied, and I nodded. "But if you ask, he might have to admit he aided us. He has already done too much."

"You make a good point," I replied, picking up my sword and wishing I still had a scabbard for it. "I seem to be ready. What do we need to gather?"

"I've already made packs for us with dried meat, bread, and skins of water," she said. "Can you reach the lantern to remove it?"

"I can," I said, doing so.

"And would you mind getting the one from my room also?" she asked, smiling.

"I begin to think you want me for my height," I replied, and she laughed sweetly. I smiled at her, but my heart wasn't in it.

When we had secured lanterns, she led me below. The boots Hugh had given me were louder than those I had lost in the tunnels, and I was obliged to move slowly so as not to make too much noise in the big, silent house. I was on the staircase down to the basement before I thought that I should have removed them. I blamed my oversight on lack of sleep and carried on.

The basement was crowded with things. I wondered that anyone could own so many things. Furniture, some of it broken, shelves lined with dusty jars, tools of various sorts, in various states of repair, and many more things than I can not remember. Eldritch led me through the piles, weaving deftly through the sometimes narrow spaces, and I wondered how she had paced it off. It was all I could do to avoid knocking one or another pile over... being a head taller than Eldritch, and having broader shoulders, made squeezing through a challenge.

Eventually she stopped before a shelf lined with the dustiest jars yet, and I watched as she carefully turned one of the lower jars. The shelf moved then, swinging open and exposing the shadowed space beyond. I opened the shutters of my lantern wide, and saw a rusty metal ladder anchored to the far side of the shallow closet-like space.

"I went below earlier," she said then. "There's a small room at the bottom with two doors, one facing south and the other east. Pentalion's tower is east of here."

"I believe so, yes."

"So we should try that one. The closer we get to his tower, the less we risk approaching it. Come, here's your pack, let's start down."

"Ladies first?" I asked, smiling.

She frowned at me and gave me a gentle push, which I suspected meant that I had better go first or she might try to make me, and I decided I had best table that joke for a while. So taking up the bundle she had prepared for me and slinging it over my shoulder, I started down.

Chapter 10: Back To The Tunnels

It was difficult going, for I had to carry my sword in my hand as I descended, and I once again wished I had its scabbard. But there was no helping it, so I made do. Eldritch followed, carrying both our lanterns by means of a cord tied to the tops of them which she had then slung over her shoulder beside her pack. I noticed her pack was smaller than mine, but then besides the obvious differences in our statures and strength, I could not deny that she ate less than I.

The descent seemed long, but eventually I alighted within the room she described. It was no more than four paces square, and did not appear to have been visited in some time. The doors were positioned as she had described, and both were of oak bound with iron. Though rusty, they still looked quite solid.

"Should I try the door?" I asked when at last Eldritch stood beside me.

"Yes, please do," she replied. "I have already looked it over, and saw no signs of any trap." I noticed, even though she had said she thought it safe, she stood well behind me and to one side as I grasped the knob with my right hand.

"It's locked," I said. "It moves a bit, so I don't think it's stuck. You will need to work your magic on it."

"Magic isn't the only solution to a locked door," she replied, handing me the lanterns. She drew small tools from her pouch, and crouching in front of the door, began to work on the lock. Very shortly I heard a click, and then she stood back up.

Taking the lanterns from me, she said, "Try it now." So I did, and found it opened easily. I pulled the door open slowly, peeking around it to see what lay beyond.

It was a corridor, a bit wider than the ones we had wandered beneath the Poor Quarter but similar in every other detail, and it lay straight as far as we could see. "Let me have a lantern, and I will enter first."

She did as I asked, and I stepped through the door. She followed a moment later, and with Eldritch again on my left we started forward.

"You never told me, Eldritch... what became of you when we were separated?"

"I nearly fell into a pit," she replied. "I felt the floor giving way beneath me and I took a leap forward, avoiding it; but once it was open I could find no way to return across it. I could hear the battle, and knew you were facing some sort of foes, but I could not join you. My spell of flight was gone by then, you see, and I lacked the power to cast another. I was considering whether or not I could cross by scaling the wall sideways when I heard someone approaching, so I became invisible."

"It was lizard men, wasn't it?"

"Yes. They probed the pit with their spears before deciding that I had somehow escaped, and then as I watched they reset the trap. Seeing how they did it revealed to me how to cross it, and as soon as I could I did. But I couldn't figure out where they had taken you. I wandered the corridors invisibly, searching for you, and I found the large room where the lizard man tribe lived. So I hid there a while, thinking they were the ones who had you, and I was right."

"So you were in the room the whole time?"

"Just so," she said. "I had little magic left, but the spell of webbing was within my power, so I bided my time until I could make it most useful."

"You did well. Without that aid I would have surely died trying to save Hugh."

The corridor was quite long. Almost by instinct I count my paces, even when speaking to someone, a habit I learned in many subterranean excursions; I had counted more than a hundred paces before we came to a fork. The corridor broke left and right at angles, and neither branch seemed to have anything to recommend it. "Which way, sorceress?"

"I think we need to bear to the north, so the left way," she replied, and so we continued on that way. The branch was as long and empty as the previous corridor, it seemed, but yet it also seemed colder. I felt a definite sense of coldness coming over me, and I began to suspect we were being followed, but a glance behind showed just our bobbing, dancing shadows.

Almost too late, I realized the danger. "Shadows!" I cried, turning suddenly and bringing both my light and my sword to bear. With the light between us and our pursuers, our own natural shadows no longer provided them cover, and I hacked at one of the monsters as soon as it was in reach. I was sure I had scored a hit, though with shadows its difficult to tell; striking a shadow with a sword feels much like striking a waterfall with one, save that you do not get wet.

Eldritch was quick to respond, doing as I had, though she was armed only with her daggers. I hoped they were enchanted, for I well knew that only a magical weapon can harm such a monster, but I knew we were not so lucky when she said, "I cannot strike them, John."

"Get behind me," I said, and as she did so I stepped in front of her. I tried to make myself take up as much of the corridor as possible as I struck another one with my sword. I felt their icy touch again, and more of my strength left me. I hacked at them crossways, felt the sword drag through their bodies, and saw them move back; in that brief moment I took a chance and placed the lantern on the floor so I could fight with both hands on my sword. "Cast a spell on them, sorceress!"

"I have no battle magic," she replied, and I knew then we could not win. But I was never one to give up without a fight.

As the monsters surged forward again, I couldn't even tell how many we faced, for their forms were so indistinct and moved about so crazily that counting them was impossible. Before they could touch me again and thus rob me of more of my strength, I swung my sword hard at the nearest. I thought I saw it fade... I hoped it wasn't my imagination.

Then they touched me again, and I jerked back away from them, feeling my sword become heavier. They were driving us backward down the unexplored corridor, and I knew that was risky. There was no telling what lay in that direction... we might back into a pit or into the lair of some monstrous creature. So I redoubled my efforts and swung once more with all my fading might.

I was sure then that I saw another of our foes fade, but they charged me again and suddenly I was too weak to stand. I crumpled to the floor under my own weight, my sword clattering useless beside me, and I knew my end was at hand.

It was not to be, not yet anyway. Eldritch stepped over me, picking up my sword. She was so brave, I thought, yet so doomed, for a woman barely five feet tall could hardly wield my four foot bastard sword. Yet wield it she did, taking one of the monsters down with one swing, suffering their icy touch as I had, then stabbing a second straight through its body. I had been sure there were more shadow monsters than that, but as she stood there over my prone form with my sword held at the ready, no more of them came forward.

"Well done," I managed to croak.

"I merely finished what you started," she replied. "There were five, and you destroyed three of them before you fell. I merely had to slay the remaining two, and one was already injured."

"How?" I said, trying to sit up. "How could you see them?"

"You could not?" she asked, looking puzzled.

"Barely," I replied. "I could see them to swing at them, but I could never have counted them so long as there were at least two."

"Curious," she replied. "Can you stand yet?"

"No," I replied, "but soon I'll be able to. I've faced these creatures before... if you survive the fight, you recover quickly."

"Well, that's good news," she replied.

"You have no battle magic?" I asked then.

"No," she replied, frowning. "I'm a thief; whenever my mistress offered me a choice of spells to learn, I naturally chose the ones I saw the most use for." She shoved my lantern toward me with her boot, then said, "I'm going to scout ahead." I was about to protest, but she continued, "Peace, John. I'll stay in sight of you."

I watched as she walked off, my sword in one hand, a lantern in the other. I could see the lantern plainly, of course, and Eldritch by its light; she went perhaps fifty more paces down the corridor, and suddenly I heard the sound of stone scraping against stone and she and her light both disappeared.

I was weak as a kitten, unable to walk. I called out "Eldritch!" in a loud voice, heedless of who or what might hear me, and began to crawl painfully forward. I was unarmed and helpless, but still determined not to lose her. I crawled the whole way, pushing the lantern ahead of me, but what I found when I got to the end was a blank wall. The passageway had turned into a dead end, and Eldritch was gone.

I dragged myself into a seated position to wait for my strength to return. I had pulled my pack behind me, and having nothing else to do, I began to look through it. Eldritch had packed crusty bread and dried meat wrapped in cloths, along with a skin which I verified was filled with water. Also in the bundle she had placed a large knife such as a cook might use, to slice the bread I assumed, but it was as big as a dagger and would serve as well. I retied the bundle without the knife inside.

By that time some of my strength had returned, and I stood up. Painstakingly I examined the wall, searching for some sign of a secret door, but I found none. It was only when I turned my attention to the walls at either side of me that I discovered a loose stone just above eye level. Assuming it to be a catch of some sort, I tried pushing it, but nothing happened.

Frustrated, I took the knife and pried at the stone, and it came out. I was still so weak that I dropped it, and only narrowly avoided it falling on my boot. Feeling around inside the hole, my fingers fell upon a cold metal rod or handle, and without a second thought I pulled it as hard as I could. But I wasn't strong enough, or it wasn't meant to be pulled. I tried again, and again, without result.

I leaned against the cold stone wall, cursing the shadow creatures who had stolen my strength, then begging whatever god might be listening to help me get it back. It was then that I heard it... a tapping, carried through the stone wall. I listened... three taps, then a pause, then three more. The pattern repeated a few times and then fell silent. Was it Eldritch? I could only hope.

I took hold of the rod once more and pulled, but it still wouldn't move. Saying a foul word, I lifted the lantern and stood on my toes to see within the hole.

Cursing myself for my foolishness, I reached inside once more and twisted the handle to the right, and then to the left, and when I tried left it moved. Stone scraped on stone, and I turned to the dead end, expectant.

It did not move. Where was that sound coming from? I looked around and saw that a door had opened behind me, in the wall beside the handle I had turned. A ragged section of the wall, barely wide enough to slip through, had swung back into a hidden chamber. Though sorely disappointed at having failed to open the way to Eldritch, I could think of nothing else to do but to enter.

It was a treasure chamber. At another time, I would have cheered. Within the small room was a large chest, a long-tailed chain shirt hanging on a metal stand, and a shortsword in a scabbard hanging from a hook beside it.

Ordinarily I would have been on the lookout for traps, but as I was in a hurry I decided some risks were called for. The first thing I did was to draw the shortsword; it gleamed in the lantern light, silver in color and entirely without rust or tarnish. I had no doubt it was magical. The armor gleamed as well, showing hints of yellow and green. The padded undershirt normally worn with chainmail was absent, but I was sure the heavy cloth shirt I was wearing would serve adequately. So I put on the armor, then buckled the sword in its scabbard to my belt.

A bit more of my strength had returned by then, but I knew I would not be able to either move the chest or to break the large padlock that secured it. Whatever was within it would have to remain there for the moment.

Besides, I still had to find Eldritch.

I restored the knife to the bundle, then managed to shoulder it. Picking up the lantern, I glanced around the room one more time, and that was when I saw the lever. It had been hidden behind the mail shirt so that I had not noticed it before. It was a small thing, with a handle that protruded only a few inches from the wall.

Without a second thought, I reached out and threw it. For a moment, nothing happened... but then I heard the scraping of stone on stone again, and as best I could I hurried out into the corridor.

I had succeeded... the wall blocking the corridor was even then sinking into the floor. Beyond it the corridor continued straight ahead... but there was no sign of Eldritch.

Well, it was too much to expect that she would stand around waiting for me to free her. I reached up and turned the hidden handle to the right, and the door to the treasure chamber closed again. I was still weak, but I was just able to lift the loose stone back into its place. A corner had chipped off, but there was nothing to do for it... the treasure would be there, or not, when I returned, and I could do nothing more to protect it.

If I returned, I reminded myself as I set out down the corridor in search of the woman I had promised not to love.

Chapter 11: Rescue

I went onward no more than twenty paces before I came to an angled intersection, where a corridor that appeared to run north and south crossed the angled corridor I was following. For a moment I was at a loss... would she have proceeded to the northeast, or turned south? The only thing I was sure about was that she would not have gone north... but neither of the other directions was exactly right.

Then I noticed an arrow, scratched into the right-hand wall of the northeastern passage. Had she made that mark, or someone else? For all I knew it might be very old indeed. But in the end, I had no other choice but to follow it.

The corridors became a veritable maze, but at each intersection I found an arrow directing me onward. I found doors and chambers and even a staircase along the way, but there also she had left arrows for me to find. At least, I hoped it was her.

I also hoped she was not using my sword to make those marks.

I was moving as fast as I felt safe, faster than she had moved I hoped, and with every step I felt a little stronger. If the arrows I followed were hers, I would surely catch up to her soon.

Then I came to an intersection without a mark.

I looked everywhere, walking down all three of the ways she might have gone ten full paces, looking high and low for any mark or sign, but there was none.

What had become of her? That she had been waylayed somehow I was sure... someone had come up behind her, or leapt out of some concealed place. Or perhaps it was one of those monsters which paralyzes... a tentacle worm, or maybe a ghoul. I ruled out the tentacle worm, as they eat their prey where it falls, but the thought that she might have been taken by a ghoul chilled my blood. The only thing I was sure about was that I had to find her, and quickly.

I remembered what Toliver had said to me many times... "It is when you hurry that you fall behind." I forced myself to be calm. How could I find her, without a sign of her passage?

I turned the key on the lantern, closing the shutters and plunging myself into the darkness. I inhaled the cool humid air of the dungeon and waited for my eyes to adjust, and I listened.

I began to think I was hearing something... a voice, maybe, some distance away. I turned toward it, and far down the corridor I was facing I saw the faintest glow; I could never have seen it with my own lantern shining.

I immediately felt a small amount of relief. Ghouls don't need light, and they generally don't speak except to gibber madly, growl, or hiss. No, I was suddenly certain that something more human was responsible for her absence.

Naturally I began to move in that direction. I was torn between the need for haste and concern that the noise of my clomping boots and my clinking armor would give me away, but shortly the need for haste took precedence and I began to trot, only slowing as I approached the source of the light.

The light issued from an arched opening in the right-hand wall of the corridor; I stopped just out of sight, for the voice was now loud enough to hear. "You're very pretty, you are. No one so pretty as you has ever been down here before. You'll like belonging to Dardith, you'll see. We will be so happy."

I decided I'd heard enough. I had the shortsword in my hand already, so I had only to step through the archway to face my foe.

The room beyond was thirty or so feet wide. Twenty or so feet from the entrance the room was divided by a wall of rusty iron bars with a gate at the right-hand end. The space before the bars was empty save for a large pile of dung and offal at the right side. The half of the room that was behind the bars was a different matter... furniture, books, clothing, and too many other ordinary items to identify in the near total darkness were arranged in precarious piles within the cell. There appeared to be a narrow cleared path just beyond the gate leading into the mess, and it was from that gap that dim light issued.

I could still hear the voice of Dardith within the pile. Though his voice was masculine, it was of a higher pitch than most and had a certain edge of madness to it. "Here, my sweet girl, let me make you more comfortable. Your cloak will be fine on this pile. Surely you don't need your boots on, do you?"

I moved quickly to the gate, only to find it locked. I had half expected it. I tried to peer within, but the cleared path curved so that I could not see far within from that angle. I could see the piles more clearly now, and noticed how dirty and shabby all the items appeared. Threadbare rugs covered the flagstone floor within right up to the gate.

I considered the situation. I could not open the gate, not without a thief or wizard, or at the very least a large prybar and several equally muscular friends, none of which I had at my command. I would have to use some subterfuge, which is not my greatest skill. I wished once more that I had Belgarett at my side, or even Argent, for his cleverness was nearly as potent as his magic. But I had neither. I did recall one piece of advice from Belgarett: "When you're surrounded by enemies and can see no way to escape, show your foe only confidence. Smile, and make it up as you go."

So I put away my sword and rattled the gate loudly. "Dardith! A word with you sir!"

"What!" he fairly screamed, and almost immediately he came in sight. Dimly lit from behind as he was, I couldn't see him very well, but I immediately noticed three things: He was holding a wand of some kind, had a dagger at his belt, and a large key hung by a chain around his neck. If he could use it, I felt sure the wand was the most significant threat, and somehow I was sure he would have no problem making it function.

I took him for an old man because of his grating voice and hunched posture, but as he approached, his pasty skin and bug eyes revealed that he had lived away from the sun for too long. He might have been only thirty or so years in truth.

I was also sure he was quite mad.

"You, there," he said as soon as he could see me. "A barbarian, eh? Come down from the north, eh? Want the girl, do you?" I noticed that though he was mad, he was careful to stand out of my reach... even if I stretched my arm through the bars, I could at most only touch him with the shortsword. I wished I still had my bow.

"She's my friend," I replied, using the same calm voice I always employed with dogs and horses.

"Not anymore!" he exclaimed. "Now she's mine!" He raised his wand, but I was quicker, turning the key of my lantern all the way open. His eyes, accustomed for many years only to the darkness underground, were dazzled by the light far more than mine were. At the same moment, I ducked. I heard him say a word I didn't know, but his wand was no longer pointed at me and so did me no harm.

I had dropped to one knee, lantern held high in my right hand in hopes that he would think I was still standing. It was at that moment that I saw what I had to do, and as quick as a striking snake I reached through the bars and pulled the rug out from under him.

I heard his head hit the floor with a loud *crack*. If he was not dead, I hoped he would still not be conscious for some time. I had only to get the key from him and I could rescue Eldritch, whom I was certain lay somewhere within the cell.

But how? He had fallen backward, and was still beyond my reach. He no longer held the wand, nor could I see it among the towering piles. I pulled on the rug experimentally, and it came away from beneath him. Evidently he had not landed fully upon it.

I heard him groan, and my heart sank. Once again time was against me... if he awakened and found his wand, he might still best me, and I could not depend on the same trick again. I unslung my pack and considered what I had to work with.

I removed my belt, then untied the cord securing the pack of supplies. I slipped the end of the belt through the buckle, then tied the end of the cord to the loose end of the belt. I had to cut a notch into the thick leather of the belt to ensure that the cord would not slip off. With that done, I reached through the bars with the belt in my left hand and the end of the cord in my right, and I threw the looped belt at Dardith's sandaled foot.

The loop fell over his foot, then slipped off as I pulled the cord. I wasted no time, for he seemed to be stirring somewhat, making a second throw as soon as I could, but this time the belt missed him entirely. Then he rolled over, trying to rise to his feet, and as he did I made one last hurried throw.

At that moment he kicked his leg up, and the looped belt slipped over his leg and tightened around his calf as I pulled. I knew the cord might not hold, but I had no choice... I hauled him toward me as fast as I could. Three strong pulls and his foot was in reach of my hand, and without delay I grabbed it and pulled it through the bars.

We struggled for several long moments, with him trying to escape my grasp and me trying to hang on. He could not be allowed to escape. Finally as he turned to try to fight me off, I grasped his arm and yanked hard, smashing his head into the bars.

I reached in with the shortsword and made sure he was dead, and only then did I take the key from his corpse.

Inside the cell I carefully worked my way through the piles of rubbish. Many were higher than my head, and the trail was almost too narrow for a man of my stature. I was concerned that I might brush against a pile and cause it to fall on me... I worried I might suffocate before I ever managed to get out.

At the center of the worthless hoard I found a roughly circular space containing a rickety-looking chair and a cot covered with filthy bedding. Eldritch lay upon the bedding, gagged, hands bound behind her back. One of her boots had been removed, and I saw her cloak folded neatly and laid upon a precarious pile against which my bastard sword also leaned. But she was lying in an unnatural position and not struggling against the ropes. For a moment I feared her dead, but then I saw her breathing slowly and realized she was paralyzed.

I considered untying her, but then the thought game to me that the filthy bedding might well be distressing her more than the ropes. "Let me get you out of here," I said. and I carefully lifted her as one lifts a newborn babe and carried her from the cell. I placed her gently in a sitting position in the corner of the outer chamber furthest from the dungheap and set about removing her gag and untying her.

When she was free of the bonds I went back into the cell and retrieved my sword, her cloak and her boot; laying her cloak and my sword beside her, I restored her boot to its proper place on her foot. "Sorceress, I have to say, I find fault with your strategy," I said as I set about buckling on my belt. "I think as soon as we have both recovered, we should leave this dungeon. I saw a staircase a little ways back which may lead out. Also, I must say I don't think much of you scouting ahead... each time you do it, something bad happens. My old friend Ularic, who was a dwarven warrior but bethought himself a minstrel, used to sing that you should never split the party."

"He... might have been right," she said slowly.

"Good, the magic is wearing off," I replied. "Perhaps shortly we can leave here."

"I agree," she said. She tried to stand, but fell forward. I reached out and caught her, then helped her up. She looked at me and said, "Thank you, John."

"You are very welcome," I said. Standing face to face with her, looking into her green elvish eyes, I could not keep the love I felt for her from my own. I thought I saw the same emotion in hers. For a long moment we stared at each other... the words were nearly on my lips, the words I wanted to say to her. *I love you.* But as I felt the words about to come out and make an oathbreaker of me, she looked away.

"I'm better now," she said, her hand pushing gently at my chest, and I let go of her and she stood on her own. "I need to find that wand. *Vedetis*." I recognized that word, having heard it many times... it was the spell of seeing magic. Her eyes sparkled and seemed almost to glow as she looked around. "You have new armor," she said, as if seeing it for the first time, "and it's enchanted."

"I was fairly sure it was," I replied. "Here, how about this sword I picked up for you?"

"It is also enchanted," she said, taking it from me. I removed the scabbard from my belt and handed it to her. "And just my size. Thank you for the loan of yours."

"I was in no condition to argue," I said, laughing. "Now perhaps if we meet shadows, you'll be appropriately armed."

"Indeed." She fastened the scabbard to her belt quickly, then turned to the open cell door. I dragged the body of Dardith out of the way and she knelt, searching the floor. Having nothing better to do, I ate some of the food in my pack. I gave a piece of bread to Eldritch, and she ate it absently while continuing her search. So I kept watch. Something told me I would not be able to convince her to give up her search.

"I found it!" she said. Turning, I saw her reaching high up on one of the piles near the gate. "He must have thrown it as he fell."

"Can you use it?" I replied.

"Of course," she said. "I don't know the spell, but I know its name. The wand will give me the power to cast it. I don't know how many times it will work, but I'd wager from the magic I can see that it will be good at least twice." Looking around, she said, "We could search here for treasure, but I doubt Dardith had anything valuable besides the wand."

"Even if he has a dragon's treasure in there, we'd be days finding it," I said. "I do not wish to remain down here any longer."

"Truth," she said. "I've lost my pack... he opened it, ate some, and scattered the rest around his... dwelling."

"We're leaving anyway, so we should be fine. I still have some left." She was looking intently at the wand, so I said, "Now you have battle magic."

"Yes," she said, smiling at me. The sparkle in her eyes was surely just the spell, but they were still captivating to me. Again she looked away after a moment. "We'd best move out."

"Wizardry," I said, shouldering my pack. "I do not understand it."

We walked out together into the corridor, with Eldritch at my left as before. "Magic seems, well, not easy, but at least understandable to me, so I do not understand those who do not understand it," she said, making me shake my head at her words. "What do you wish to know?"

"Well," I said, "I could go about saying 'laflictis' all day long and my feet would never leave the ground. What makes the word work for you?"

She laughed at my foolishness. "And I could go about saying 'dephlotis' all day long and yet arrows would not turn away from me. The word isn't the spell, it's just the key to the magic."

"I would say that I see, but I do not see at all."

She sighed then. "A wizard must study, sometimes for days, to learn a single spell. When the framework of the spell is in a wizard's mind, a word is needed to call it forth. And so we use words bastardized from the ancient Thailish as keys."

We reached the unmarked intersection and turned back the way we had come. "Now perhaps I see a little bit," I said. "But why then do wizards keep those heavy spellbooks, when the magic is within them?"

"Spells not used rust like weapons left untended. If I wish to use one I've not cast in a while, I may find I need to refresh my memory."

"And what of those who do magic by chanting?" I asked.

She grimaced. "Chanting is for demon-summoners and priests, and as far as I'm concerned, there is little difference between them."

"Eldritch!" I exclaimed, once again shocked at her blasphemy. "How is it that the gods do not strike you down?"

"The gods. Bah. They do not care about me. They care so little that I am not even worth the effort of a good curse. And if they do not care about me, why then should I care about them?"

Troubled to my very soul, I could not find an answer for her. Instead, I just shook my head. "The staircase is just ahead," I said. "I'll go first."

"You're learning," she said, a hint of laughter in her voice. Still troubled, I did not reply, but merely started up the narrow steps.

Chapter 12: Sanctuary

The staircase was long, perhaps as much as three stories with no turns or landings. At the top it ended in a stone-walled space big enough for just one of us to stand, and as I had gone up first Eldritch was obliged to stand on the steps.

The compartment had a low ceiling, low enough that I had to crouch slightly. There was a sort of a wooden hatch recessed into the wall at my left, starting at about my waist level and reaching almost to the ceiling, not quite three feet wide. It was held by a peculiar catch, a brass hook gone green with age attached to an axle projecting from the stone frame; the hook was latched into a sort of a staple attached to the door. It appeared an easy enough matter to lift the hook and open the door. "Shall I take a peek?" I whispered.

"Yes, do," replied Eldritch quietly. So I lifted the hook slowly, holding the staple with my other hand so that the door would not pop open suddenly, and then I let the door open a little and looked out.

"I know this place," I whispered, and without waiting for Eldritch to look I let the door open the rest of the way and crawled out. Turning, I offered a hand to her, but she did not take it.

"This is a temple," she said disapprovingly as I secured the hatch. It was set into the wood-paneled base beneath one of the pillars near the sanctuary, and when it was closed no one would know it was there. I did not know where the hidden catch was that would open it from the outside, but it didn't matter to me as I had no intention of returning through it.

"Yes," I said quietly. "This is the Reformer temple where I came to report the passing of Brother Radric. Better yet, it is only a street away from Pentalion's tower, so your plan did work out after all."

I looked upon the large open space with its high vaulted roof, twin colonnades, and massive stone altar. The windows were of glass, stained in a simple pattern of green and blue and yellow, and long hangings of simple brown fabric framing the holy symbol behind the altar were the only other decorations. The space was at once rustic and majestic, both like and unlike the various temples of the Hundred Gods I knew from my youth. I breathed it in, and it felt good.

"Oh, my," came a male voice from behind me. I turned about and saw a man in the brown robes of a priest. "I didn't hear you come in."

"Father Baynard," I said, extending my right hand. He took it, and I said, "Do you remember me?"

"I do," he said, dawning comprehension on his face. "You are John Northcrosse, friend of our departed Brother Radric. You are not a member of our flock but an honorable man no less. But who is this with you?"

"This is Eldritch, my friend." Father Baynard held out his hand, and after a long moment Eldritch took it without enthusiasm. "She stands accused with me of murder in the house of Pentalion."

"I see," he said. "Have you come seeking sanctuary?"

"Perhaps," I replied. "Tell me, Father, do you believe us guilty?"

"Of a crime in the house of Pentalion?" he replied. "No. I have long suspected him of various sins, and though judgement is the privilege of Tah still I find you more honorable than he. I would hear your side of it, if you will tell me."

"I will," I said. "Eldritch and I each independently determined that the missing girls in the Poor Quarter were the work of Pentalion. With a bit of magic and a clever trick I entered the tower, killing a hobgoblin guard in the process. Eldritch and I met shortly thereafter in a battle with more of his hobgoblin guards, and yes, we killed them also."

"You know that hobgoblins are the children of Tah just as men are," he said, reproachfully.

"Even so, they were complicit in the abduction of the girls. We discovered that Pentalion kept a strange beast, a kind of hydra, in the dungeon beneath the tower, and that he fed the girls alive to the monster for his own amusement. I witnessed some of the hobgoblins conferring with their master in the presence of a bound and gagged girl, whom we saved."

"I concede your point," he said, "recalling once again that judgement is the privilege of Tah and therefore not my place. So what of this monster?"

"We slew it," I said, "but by his magic Pentalion has hidden all sign of its existence. It is truly his word against ours."

"I believe you," he said. "Come, let me take you to my chambers, where you can rest." I followed him, and after a moment Eldritch followed me. He took us through a side door and into his apartments which were attached to the temple as a sort of wing. The furnishings were simple and rustic, with little in the way of decoration as befits a believer of the Reformed Church of Tah. He settled us in a sort of parlor which held several comfortable chairs and small tables. "You are hurt," he said as I lowered myself into a chair.

"I have bruises, and a small wound on my hip." In truth just then I was feeling every injury keenly; every bruise, the goose-egg on the back of my head, my wounded hip and even the residual soreness in my shoulder.

Without asking, he laid one hand on my shoulder and held the other up toward the heavens, and said, "Tah, O mighty god, have mercy on this honorable man, friend of our Brother and of the poor. Let your sublime grace flow through me. Heal his wounds that he may carry on his work." I felt the pain flow out of me like water running from a duck's back, to be replaced with a pleasant warmth, and I knew if I looked that all sign of my injuries would be gone.

"Now let me get some tea," he said, and before I could protest that he should not serve me further he had slipped through an inner door and was gone.

All this time Eldritch had stood near the doorway through which we had entered. I said, "Rest, sorceress, for we may not get rest again soon."

She sat down then, leaning forward as if unwilling to accept comfort from even a chair within the temple of Tah.

"Tell me, sorceress," I said. "Tell me why you hate priests so much."

She almost glared at me. "When I was a novice thief, nine winters old, I had a friend named Nix. He was younger than I, but I looked younger than he. We were working the market near the canal, cutting purses and stealing fruit; usually we had an older thief as trainer, but we had gone without permission that day to practice on our own."

She paused, eyes downcast, and after a moment I said, "If this is too difficult, you need not speak of it."

"No, I'm alright," she replied, turning her reddened eyes to me. "One of his marks caught him, took his knife and stabbed him in the gut. I saw it happen, and I rushed to his side. We tried to return to the house where we were living in the Poor Quarter, but he was bleeding so much, and when he fell in an alleyway I could not lift him." She stopped a moment, overcome, wiping tears from her eyes. "We were right beside a temple, so I ran inside and found a priest, and told him what had happened. He looked at me coldly, and said, 'Thief, do not defile this temple with lies. Go, and do not return.'"

She stood up then and paced back and forth a few moments, arms folded, and I waited patiently. Finally she said, "So I went back to Nix, and he died in my arms."

I stood up and put my arms around her, though she kept hers folded between us, and I said, "I sense there is more to the story, Eldritch, but if you do not wish to tell it I will not ask."

She pushed me away, gently. "The abandoned temple where I was living?" she said, and I nodded. "It was that temple. I ruined them. They called me a thief, so I visited the temple by night, stealing everything; I took their money and their golden holy symbols and implements, over and over. They tried everything to stop me, but I was determined... every way they blocked, I opened, and everything they hid I found.

There came a day when the priests all left, and I declared victory. Later when Melora died I found the temple still empty, for many thought it cursed. I knew I was the only curse upon it, so I took it as my residence."

"Ahem," said Father Baynard. "I'm sorry, I didn't mean to eavesdrop." He looked at Eldritch deeply, his eyes sad. "My child, I'm sorry you lost your friend because a priest judged you. Please don't think we are all like that."

"It doesn't matter," she yelled at him, tears streaking her angry face, her fists clenched. "The gods do not care for me. No god loves me. Everyone I ever loved, the gods took from me! My mother, Nix, Melora, all of them and more have been taken. I fear no god's curse because I am already cursed!" She sat down then and buried her face in her hands.

I could only watch, helpless. Now I knew why she lived alone, and I marveled that she ever let me into her home.

A bell rang, startling me. "Oh, dear," said Father Baynard, "I have visitors. Please, John, you and your friend feel free to remain here." With that he left through the door to the main temple.

I turned back to Eldritch. She had somehow composed herself. Her face was still wet with tears, and her eyes red, but she had an expression of calm on her face. "Eldritch, I..." I began, but she interrupted me.

"No, John," she said. "Not now. Now we have other problems to attend to."

I was about to speak further when I realized I was hearing a woman weeping. Curiosity and compassion overcame decorum as I moved to the door and opened it just enough to see and hear.

Father Baynard was standing in the middle of the temple talking to a man and a woman. From their clothing I assumed he was a merchant or artisan, and she his wife. Both were in tears; the woman was so overwrought that she could not speak, but her husband was speaking to the priest.

"... the window was open, Father, and she was gone. We told the watch but they said she ran away. She didn't run away! Kimbery was a good girl, we loved her, she was happy. Why would she run away?"

"Peace, my son," said Father Baynard. "Was there any sign left of whomever might have taken her?"

"Just this," said the man, holding something out to the priest. I opened the door all the way so I could see it better.

In his hand was a doll. A doll wearing a jacket of blue fabric, with a single tarnished silver button affixed to it.

I strode purposefully into the temple. "Good man, I know who has your daughter," I said, "and with your leave we will try to win her freedom."

"Who are you?"

"John Northcrosse, at your service," I said. "You may have seen my face on a wanted poster or two around town." He looked then as if he were about to run for the door, and his wife seemed likely to precede him, so I said, "Peace. I mean you no harm. We are wanted for murder within the tower of Pentalion, but I tell you now that we murdered only hobgoblins and rescued a young girl he had taken." I reached out and took the doll from his nerveless fingers. "I'll need this to deal with him, but trust me when I say that I will deal with him, or die trying."

"I... um... thank you, sir," he said, and I nodded.

"We must prepare, for the day grows short," I said. "Father Baynard will contact you upon our return with Kimbery." I didn't wait for any reply, but turned immediately back toward the room where Eldritch waited.

I saw that she was watching from the doorway as I had, and as she opened it for me I handed her the doll. "Pentalion took another girl, and left this as his calling card."

"It's a trap," she replied, "baited for us."

"How did he know we would be here? Indeed, how did he know they would come here?"

"Perhaps he has some divination magic I'm not aware of," she replied. "It doesn't matter. He has set a trap for us that he knows we cannot honorably avoid."

"So we won't," I replied. "We know it's a trap. He has his magic, a company of mercenaries, and a hostage. We have my sword, and your magic. So we go in the front door and make things up as we go along."

"That's a terrible strategy," she replied. "We're sure to fail."

"Tah believes in you, child, even if you don't believe in him," said Father Baynard, entering from the temple.

"Bah," she said. "I'll do it, John, because I believe in you, not because I believe in Tah."

"Did you send the girl's parents home?" I asked.

"No. They are praying for your success." He smiled. "As will I when you have gone. I cannot condone violence, but I can pray that both you and the girl Kimbery will emerge unharmed."

"Thank you," I said. Eldritch stood with arms crossed, but did not speak further. "We won't need all the things we arrived here with."

"Leave your things here," he said. "I'll see to them." So I left the bundle and the lantern I'd been carrying. Eldritch left her lantern as well, but I saw her tuck the doll into her pouch.

I laid my sword over my shoulder and walked out into the late afternoon light. This time Eldritch walked at my right, so that we could bring weapons to bear on all sides. The people on the streets parted before us as though we were royalty, and very shortly we came in sight of our foe's stronghold.

I saw mercenaries in Pentalion's red surcoats arrayed around the tower, close enough so that each could see at least two others. Four stood guard before the main entrance, and I approached them directly.

"Halt," said one of them who I took for a junior officer. "Who are you, and why do you approach the tower of Pentalion."

I smiled broadly. "If you do not know who I am, then your master should dismiss you. We are expected... make way."

He frowned, but did not speak further. Instead he gave a curt wave, and stepped aside; two others opened the doors, and after we had entered the corridor the doors were closed behind us.

Eldritch and I stood alone in the wide front corridor of Pentalion's tower. Unlike the back corridor, the one in which we stood had double doors at each end but no side doors at all. "They did not follow," I said. "Can those within be that confident?"

"Perhaps," she replied, looking me in the eyes. For a long moment we just looked at each other, and then she grabbed the front of my mailshirt and pulled my face down to hers. She gave me a fierce kiss that fanned the flames within me; I had only begun to respond when she broke away. "For luck, swordsman," she said, her face flushed.

"Luck, sorceress," I said, and with weapons ready we strode toward the inner doors together.

Chapter 13: Into The Lair

The doors opened as we approached them, and we entered into the circular central room of Pentalion's tower. The well which had dominated the room before was still closed magically, leaving the bare flagstone floor unbroken across its entire sixty foot diameter. The sourceless light revealed that the circular wall was lined with mercenaries; I didn't count them, as I didn't care to know my odds exactly. At the far side of the room Pentalion sat in a large, comfortable chair placed a few paces in front of the back door. Beside him stood Grantier, smirking.

For the barest moment I felt despair gnawing at the edges of my soul, but I remembered again Belgarett's advice. Letting a broad grin spread across my face, I laid my sword over my shoulder and assumed a casual pose.

"I knew you would come," said Pentalion, his soft voice carrying surprisingly well in the otherwise silent room.

"How could we refuse?" I replied. "You sent us a personalized invitation."

"Where's the girl?" asked Eldritch, her voice serious.

"Why, she's right here," replied the wizard, raising his hand in a waving motion. One of the mercenaries opened the rear door, and the girl ran out and knelt beside Pentalion's chair. Absently he stroked her hair as she looked up at him reverently.

"Karistos," said Eldritch under her breath. "She's charmed."

Grantier stepped forward then. "John Northcrosse, we meet at last."

"I'd say it was a pleasure, but I'd be lying," I replied.

"They say that those who use huge swords are trying to make up for a shortfall in a more personal area," he replied, smirking broadly at his jest. Some of the mercenaries ringing the room chuckled, and he allowed it for a moment before silencing them with a look.

"Do I hear you rightly?" I said. "You seek to impugn my manhood?"

"I think it impugns itself," he replied, and again there were chuckles.

"Such an insult is unacceptable to warriors of my people," I said, suddenly serious. He had given me an opportunity, and I meant to take hold of it. "I seem to recall that it is the same among yours. So it is my right to challenge you to a duel."

I saw the look on his face... he recognized his mistake. If he backed down now, he would lose the confidence of his men; but if he accepted, he would have to duel me fairly. I knew I could not defeat all his men, but I felt I had a fair chance to defeat him by himself.

"You have a sorceress by your side," he said.

"She knows the code of dueling," I replied. "Besides, you have a wizard of your own. Eldritch, stand back and keep your eyes on Pentalion. This must be an honest duel."

Grantier knew he could not avoid dueling me. He put on his best smirk and stepped forward a few paces, posing as casually as I did. Pentalion was glaring at the mercenary captain's back, obviously very angry at his foolishness.

I considered our relative strengths. Grantier wore better armor than I, and had a shield. I was taller and longer-limbed, and my sword was a foot longer than his. Further, he was facing a left-handed warrior... his shield would be less useful against me than against a right-handed opponent. He had a mighty reputation, but modesty aside I knew myself to be a capable swordsman as well.

Finally I assumed a ready position, sword in one hand, and I said, "I am John Northcrosse! I have fought men and monsters from the Demonfrost Mountains to the Desert of Nol. I have won a drinking contest with a dwarf, and a debate with an elf, and I have eaten the heart of a dragon. I do not fear you."

A few of the mercenaries chuckled nervously. Grantier raised his sword to ready and crouched, and we began to circle, looking for an opening. I did not like showing my back to the wizard, knowing that he was likely the least honorable man in the room, but even as I made the turn I could see Eldritch watching him like a hawk from the sidelines. The mercenaries had stepped aside, leaving her space to stand alone before the closed front doors.

"A real warrior does not boast of his success," said Grantier at last, and he charged forward. "His successes speak for themselves!"

The next few moments were a blur, as he rained attacks on me like a spring storm come down from the mountains. I intercepted every blow with such speed that it seemed the sword moved on its own. I could not think, only respond, and I knew if he kept up his onslaught he would land a blow eventually.

He drove me backward a few steps, and I turned and began to circle. It would be a bad idea to approach the men standing near the walls, for I could not trust that they would be truly honorable when tempted by easy prey.

Grantier's attacks slowed, and I saw that he had overextended himself in hopes of ending me quickly. Had I been a lesser warrior, he might well have succeeded.

Now I pressed the attack, using my greater reach to strike at his sword arm, forcing him to turn his shield toward me. In such a position he could not attack me at all, and now I pressed forward, thrusting with my sword rather than swinging it, driving him backward in turn. With that approach I achieved first blood, wounding his left leg when he failed to completely turn aside one of my strikes.

I took care not to overextend myself, for I felt sure he was looking for that and would quickly close with me if I gave him the chance. After I wounded him, he seemed to redouble his efforts, and with a trick of swordplay I'd not seen before he slipped his blade inside my guard and stabbed my left shoulder.

Such a wound could be disastrous for me, and he knew it. A wide grin spread across his face, signaling his expectation of victory. But the wound was not bad; though it would weaken me in time, for the moment it was a minor thing. I went on the offensive again immediately, catching him by surprise, and though he deflected my thrust he could not avoid the backhanded slash I made at him afterward. My enchanted sword slipped between the plates of the armor protecting his knee, cutting through the mail underneath, and I saw blood on my blade as I drew it back.

He was not crippled, but he was slowed, and it was my turn to smile. I could see by the look on his face that he knew his doom was at hand as we again began to trade blows. I took my sword in both hands and pushed him, driving him backward. His wound was making him slow, and I knew I needed to take advantage of his weakness before my own wound began to tell on me.

There came a moment when he took a step backward and almost stumbled, and I made my move, reaching long inside his guard and sweeping him from his feet with my sword. He fell heavily on his back, and I leapt forward and planted my boot on his sword, placing the tip of mine at his throat.

I was about to command him to yield when I heard the wizard's soft voice in the sudden quiet... "*Karistos.*"

Pentalion was my friend, had always been my friend. What was I doing, fighting with Grantier, the man my friend had hired to defend him? I took a step back, freeing the mercenary captain's sword, and looked at my friend Pentalion. I was hoping he would guide me, to help me figure out what was going on.

I saw him stroking the hair of the little girl, Kimbery. She was young, perhaps seven or eight years, blonde and pretty, and an image of another girl bound to a stone altar came into my mind. In that image, Pentalion stood over her with a wicked knife.

It was as if there were two men in my head then... one who loved Pentalion as one loves his father, and the other who knew what a monster he was. They were evenly matched, and so I stood with my head in one hand, my sword-tip dragging the floor as I shuffled backwards. I heard a sound and looked up to see Grantier standing, sword in hand, a grim expression on his face. Part of me screamed in impotent rage, trying to raise my sword, while the other refused to believe he posed a threat.

A woman's voice said "*Intere-* oof!" I turned dumbly to look and saw Eldritch lying face-down on the floor. Someone had pushed her down, or perhaps stabbed her, I couldn't tell. I didn't know if she was alive or dead.

The vision in my head changed. The girl on the altar was Eldritch, and the wizard's monster was rising up behind her. Her face was turned toward me in entreaty, and I remembered then my love for her, a love not made of magic but of something more sublimely powerful.

Grantier rushed at me, even as I began to overcome the wizard's spell. I could not make my hand raise my sword... he would kill me if I didn't, but I felt like my mind was moving through deep snow. Then I heard Eldritch say, "*Fralineen,*" and the floor shuddered beneath us.

Grantier stumbled for a moment, and I tore the remaining cobwebs from my mind and lifted my sword high. We traded blows again, fiercely, for each of us knew no quarter would be asked or given now. We were both injured, my injury limiting my reach, his limiting his quickness, and so we were again evenly matched... but I had a smile on my face, for I knew what Eldritch had done while my foeman did not. I heard Pentalion and Eldritch both speaking magic words, but I couldn't make out what they were saying nor spare a glance to see. Keeping Grantier busy and preventing him from seeing the danger he was in was all that I could do. My task was made more difficult when several of the mercenaries began to be yell a warning at him; thankfully the noise of our battle drowned them out.

When the moment came that I could finally press my secret advantage, I feinted to his right, and as he parried my blow I raised my right boot and kicked his shield hard, forcing him to step backwards.

Into the well. Eldritch's spell had caused the well in the floor to begin to open... the well was three or four paces across already and still growing. The sound of his impact on the stone floor far below told me my enemy was surely dead.

At that selfsame moment I heard a cry, and I looked for the source of the sound. It was Eldritch, hovering in the air before Pentalion, her hand on the shortsword protruding from his chest. It had been his outcry I had heard. His mouth was working, opening and closing like a fish, and then he croaked out

"*Thalactis!*" and disappeared. In a frozen moment I saw a drop of his blood fall from her sword-tip.

"Damn," I said, raising my sword once again. The mercenaries were on the move now, closing with us, and one of them leaped toward Eldritch. His outstretched sword missed her as she flew up toward the arching ceiling out of his reach. Most of the others were moving in on me; without an ally at my back, I knew I would not last long enough to recite my boast again.

"Mercenaries!" I called out. "Your leader lies dead! He would have taken my life by treachery. Are you all so dishonorable as he? Look, see the girl Pentalion would have slain!" She was crouching, terrified, behind the chair, and I well understood her confusion and her fear. "Do you really think he would give her back to her parents unharmed? I tell you now, she was not the first child he took, and her fate would have been as bloody as the rest had we not come."

They had stopped to hear me out. Now several of them turned away, sheathing their swords and walking toward the front doors, and for a moment I thought they all would. But then one of them, a large man with a small cruel eyes, cried out, "Hold, all of you! Will you listen to this barbarian? He slew our captain... we are bound by honor to avenge him!"

He only succeeded in rallying five of his comrades to his cause, but that was four more of them than I felt ready to battle, and I could see they were not going to let me fight them one at a time. The only fortune I had was that the well prevented most of them from moving directly toward me, so that I had time to back up toward the wall. At least they wouldn't be able to flank me.

The battle was joined before I reached the wall, and my new chainshirt proved its worth by deflecting several of their blows as my sword flew about deflecting others. Still, I could not fight them all forever.

I heard Eldritch's voice then. "Inforzala!" There was something different, somehow, about how she said it, but it was effective nonetheless as one of my opponents fell to the floor like a puppet with its strings cut. My grin returned as I continued to defend myself. Another of my opponents turned, looking for the source of the magical attack, only to see Eldritch flying out of his reach. She said the word again, and another of my foes fell, for she was ignoring the one facing her. After all, he could do nothing against her.

Now I had but two opponents, one being he who had rallied them against me. His face was grim, and I knew he would not stop until I was dead or he was unable to continue. I hoped Eldritch would turn the wand on him next.

She said the word again, then cried out in pain, and I saw her falling. The man who had been facing her now lay stretched out on the floor. Concern for her gave me new strength, and I delivered a fatal slash to the neck of my lesser foeman.

Drawing back my sword, I said to my remaining enemy, "What is your name, mercenary?"

"Leuric is the name of the man who will slay you," he said, smiling.

"Good," I said, parrying a blow he had aimed at my face. Recovering, I said, "I'll be sure to put that on your tombstone," and as he raised his sword for another cut at my head I brought my sword two-handed against his side, chopping through the mail and spilling his blood and guts on the floor. As he fell to his knees I said, "Tell Grantier I said hello when you reach the netherworld." He fell over backwards, and all was quiet in the room but for the soft crying of Kimbery, still hiding behind the wizard's chair.

I ran to Eldritch, who had fallen to the floor beside the well. Another pace toward the center of the room and she would have laid beside Grantier. I saw then why she had fallen... there was a dagger protruding from her belly. "He threw it," she said. "I thought he couldn't hurt me, so I ignored him and tried to save you instead."

"You did," I said, tears welling up in my eyes. "You saved me." She fumbled for the dagger, but I said, "No, no, don't pull it out. We have to get you to a healer."

"No. No priests," she said. Putting one arm around my neck, she pulled my face down to hers and kissed me, gently. "Lisset," she whispered.

"What?"

"Lisset," she said again. "It's my name. The one my... mother gave me." Her eyes fell closed then, and I felt sure they would not open again.

Chapter 14: Resolutions

"Son, move aside," came a voice from above me. I looked up in amazement to see Father Baynard. I laid

Eldritch... Lisset... down on the floor gently and moved back. He laid his hand on her belly so that his thumb and fingers framed the dagger, and he said, "Tah, O loving god, have mercy on this woman who has done your will today. Grant your humble servant the power to heal her wound that she may live to serve you again." At the end of the prayer he drew out the weapon, and her chest heaved as she drew a deep breath.

It was then that I realized I had forgotten to breathe myself. I took a ragged breath and looked around. I saw Kimbery's parents at her side, comforting her, while watchmen moved around the room, some securing the mercenaries while others seemed to be just looking around. I expected any moment that they would turn their attention to me, and when one approached I stood up and faced him squarely.

He took off his helmet and I saw that it was Hugh. "John Northcrosse," he said, smiling, "you left without saying goodbye."

"I'm sorry," I replied. "We worried you might be held to account for helping us."

"Ah. So that's why you stole food and lanterns from me." He laughed, and I laughed with him.

"Father Baynard has your lanterns," I replied. "We did intend to return them as time permitted."

"It is nothing," he said.

"You may take me in now," I said. "I am ready to surrender."

"Surrender?" he said, mischief in his voice. "Why would you surrender?" He saw my confusion, and took pity on me. "My parents returned, John, and I told them all you had told me. My mother is good friends with the wife of the Chief Magistrate, and so word was passed to him that you and your friend were falsely accused. He was not prepared to order us into the tower, and honestly so long as Pentalion remained a threat I do not think I could have convinced any of my men to enter, so we merely surrounded the tower and waited to see what would transpire. When mercenaries came out saying that Pentalion had disappeared after suffering what might be a fatal wound, I convinced the most courageous of my men to follow me."

"Your men?"

"Oh, yes, that," he said, indicating the insignia on his shoulder. I did not yet understand the marks used in Slateholm, and it showed on my face. "I'm not a second lieutenant anymore," he continued. "I've been promoted to first lieutenant now, and owing to recent shortage of captains I now lead half the watchmen in the Merchant's Quarter."

"It couldn't have happened to a more deserving warrior," I said, clapping him on the shoulder.

"Swordsman," said Eldritch, and I turned and saw her standing by my side. Father Baynard came toward us before she could speak further, leading Kimbery and her parents, and the latter two hugged us and cried on us and thanked us for saving their daughter. Her father wanted to pay us, but I refused him. I saw irritation on Eldritch's face when I did that, and I could only smile at her foolishly. I well knew what she was thinking, but I also knew something she did not, and I would not take money from this working man if I could avoid it.

They left then, leaving Hugh, Father Baynard, Eldritch, and myself standing together. Eldritch looked at the priest darkly for a moment, then said, "Father Baynard, I... thank you. Thank you for saving me, even though I spoke ill of your god."

"You are welcome, child," he said. "Forgiveness is the duty of the true follower of Tah, as Tah himself forgives those who seek him."

"I'm not ready for that," she said.

"Give it time," he replied, turning away before she could protest further. At that same moment, one of Hugh's men called his attention to something, and Eldritch and I were left alone.

"John," she said quietly, "what I told you before... that was for you only."

"As I expected," I replied. "All your secrets are safe with me."

"Why did you turn that man down when he wanted to pay us?" she said then, her mood swiftly changing to irritation again. Before I had a moment to answer, I saw her face change yet again, from irritation to concern. "We have nothing left between us."

"Peace, sorceress," I said. "Hugh! A moment of your time."

"Yes?" he said, returning to us where we stood beside the well.

"Tell me, now that Pentalion is revealed as a child kidnapper, who owns this place?"

"By the laws of Slateholm, the Prince will take possession of it," he replied. "But between you and I, whatever isn't nailed down is fair game until dawn tomorrow, for it is already sunset; none of my men will remain here after dark."

We spent the night looting the wizard's tower. What we found was surprisingly little for such a powerful man. A few hundred crowns, some fine silverware, a few items of jewelry. It seemed his wealth was in the form of artwork, fine furnishings, and a laboratory full of glassware and complicated alchemical devices. Eldritch never found Pentalion's spellbooks, but in a library on the third floor she found the spellbooks of Melora and Tiberius Zara, and lying on the library table was her own. Her joy at finding all those spellbooks was wonderful to see, and in her excitement she turned to me and kissed me.

I returned her kiss once again, expecting at every moment that she would push me away, but she did not, not for a long time. When at last she did, she looked up into my eyes and said, "John Northcrosse, I can't deny it anymore. I love you. It is wrong, all wrong for me, and we both know it, but it doesn't matter to my heart. I'll never be able to resist you."

Her face darkened then, sadness stealing over her features which had just been radiant with love. "Lisset, dear Lisset," I said, "I know you now. You fear my loss. Everyone you ever loved has been taken from you, and you fear I will be also." I saw tears welling up in her eyes, but she did not try to push away from my embrace as I half expected her to. "I can't promise you nothing will ever take me from you. No mortal can make that promise. But I can promise you this... with neither friendship nor love, your life will be empty." I wanted to say more, but I stopped myself, for I was perilously close to breaking my oath to her.

She buried her face in my mailshirt, crying, and I held her to me. At length she said, "You are right, swordsman. I'm sad now, but I've been so much sadder, and yet I'm happier now than I've ever been." She turned her brilliant green eyes up to me again. "I love you."

I grinned at her. "I would reply in kind, but I am no oathbreaker."

"You!" she said. Pushing me away, she stood very formally and said, "John Northcrosse, I release you from your oath to me."

"I love you, Lisset," I said. "I will always love you, so long as I live." I reached out then and pulled her to me, and we kissed again.

At length I paused to remove my mailshirt, and she said to me, "John, I... I've never..."

"And I have," I said gently, caressing her cheek. "Does that trouble you?"

"No," she said. "We both have pasts, and I accept that. I just wanted you to know..."

I smiled. "Are you asking me to be gentle with you, sorceress?"

"No," she said, showing me a sweet smile tinged with mischief I'd never seen on her before. "Go slow with me, swordsman. But you don't need to be particularly gentle."

My shirt followed my mailshirt to the floor. I pulled her to me, reaching for the buttons of her green silk shirt, and she said, "Are we going to use the library table, then?"

"It seems sturdy enough," I replied, slapping it firmly.

She showed me that smile again and said, "Why don't we try a different room? One more appropriately furnished, perhaps?"

"Lisset, wherever you lead me, I will follow." And I did.

As the sun rose we stood together at the front door of the Hedgekin house. I knocked, and shortly we were led into the presence of Hugh and his father Heral, to whom Hugh introduced us. We shook their hands, and Heral invited us to breakfast with them, so we did. Heral's wife Olivet joined us briefly, but when Heral asked us to tell him about the previous day's battle she left, saying "I'm sorry, but I cannot abide violence." So we told our story to the two men, and afterward Heral excused himself, encouraging Eldritch and I to remain as long as we wished.

I took a long drink of the fresh fruit juice which had been provided to me, well aware that both Hugh and Eldritch were looking at me curiously across the kitchen table. Finally she said, "Well, out with it, swordsman! I can see that you are bursting to tell us something."

I turned to face her, saying, "You recall how we found the secret door in the basement here?" As she nodded, Hugh leaned forward, suddenly very interested. "And you recall the place where you and I were separated, after the shadows attacked?" Again she nodded, and I continued, "Near that point I found a secret chamber, and within it my mailshirt, your shortsword, and a chest. Well, so far as I know, the chest is still there, and I know we three together can easily retrieve it. What say you?"

"Aye!" they both exclaimed, and so we began to make plans for our descent. But that is another story...

Djinn

It was a hot night in Iraq, as nights there often are, but not as hot as the preceding day. I had stayed late at the dig site to finish packing away the day's finds in the relative coolness. With no one around to hear me, I took great pleasure (however childish) in calling each artifact a different foul name.

It would be fair to say I wasn't happy on the expedition. I was a computer science major, not an archaeologist at all... I wouldn't have even signed up if I hadn't fallen for a pretty girl who happened to be the archaeology professor's pet. But I discovered too late that she wasn't really all that interested in me. So there I was, digging in the hard packed dirt in the desert heat for artifacts, in the ruins of a village so minor that the professor himself said "No one rich or important ever lived here," and worse, cataloging the worthless items we found with a pencil and paper because the professor didn't believe in computers.

I reviewed the check-in list, and concluded that the only item left was an ugly pot someone had dug up late in the day. Looking around, I didn't see it. Muttering to myself, I laid the clipboard down on the ruined wall that, before we began digging, was the only sign a village had ever stood there, and began searching for the pot.

Just as I caught sight of it, I heard a clatter behind me. Turning, I saw by the light of the nearly-full moon and the scattered solar lanterns that the clipboard was no longer on the wall. It had fallen off into the dig site. I said a few choice words, then picked up a lantern and went looking for it. I imagined the papers had all gone flying, and figured I was in for an extra hour or so trying to find them all and put them back in order.

Shining my light down into the pit, I was relieved to see that the clipboard had landed with all the papers still firmly clamped in place. Unfortunately, it had fallen into the deepest part of the dig. I would have to climb down after it.

The next thing I knew, I was falling, and almost before that fact had registered in my mind, I hit the bottom with a jolt. I lay there in the dark for a moment, catching my breath. The floor of the pit had given way beneath me, I realized, dropping me into a narrow hole a couple of meters deep. It was dark... the lantern had gone out in the fall. Feeling around for it, I managed to cut my hand on an improbably sharp piece of broken plastic. Cursing some more, I proceeded more carefully, trying to figure out how big the hole was and if I could somehow climb out.

My hands landed on a bottle, half buried in the dirt and debris I had brought down from above. It was twenty or so centimeters long and not very heavy, so though it was stoppered and sealed I assumed it must be empty.

I stood up carefully and felt above me, and found the edge of the hole. *Good,* I thought, *I can get out of here.* I picked up the bottle carefully and lifted it out, then climbed out after it. I was extra careful as I returned to the surface, what with only having moonlight to see by while trying to hang on to the clipboard and the mysterious bottle at the same time.

I placed the bottle on one of the crates I had been filling, and examined it by the light of another lantern. It was made of a red translucent glass, shaped a bit like a slender flower vase, and it seemed to be empty. As I've said, I'm no archaeology student, but I could see it wasn't the same sort of work as the other ugly things we'd been pulling out of the ground.

I knew I shouldn't mess with it, I should just catalog it like everything else, but curiosity got the better of me. With my pocket knife I pried the hard wax away from the stopper and pulled it out.

At this point in the story, you'd be expecting me to tell you about smoke rolling out of the bottle, but it wasn't like that at all. There was just this perfume that suddenly filled the air. It was a very nice fragrance... a feminine fragrance, old and rich.

"I am yours to command," came a voice, and I nearly jumped out of my shoes. Standing very close to me was a woman. She was beautiful, curvaceous yet girlish, with dark hair and dark eyes that sparkled in the moonlight. She was clothed in a silk gown that was adequately modest to my Western eyes but which would have scandalized the locals, and lightly-made slippers of the same material.

It took me a moment to find my voice. Finally I said, "Who are you?"

"I am the djinn of the bottle," she said. "You have released me, and so you are to be granted three wishes."

"Wishes?" I asked, hardly comprehending. "This is like some storybook. No, it's a dream. That's what it is, a dream. I've hit my head in that pit, and I'm passed out down there right now dreaming this."

She smiled. "I assure you, I am real." She held out a hand, palm up, and I reached out and laid my hand on top of it before I realized what I was doing. Her hand was warm and soft and very pleasant to touch. And very, very real.

"Wishes," I said. The surprise was fading, and I couldn't help but believe. "I've read about djinns and wishes. If I make a wish, will you grant me what I want, or will you try to twist the meaning of my words to torment me?"

"I might do either," she said, smiling sweetly. "It would depend on whether or not I approve of your wish. A wish that offends me, I might well turn against you, but a wish more in line with my tastes I might grant just as you hope I would."

"I see," I said. "So... what do you desire? What sort of wish might you approve of?"

"I... cannot say," she said, slowly. "It is not permitted."

"So. If I make a wish you approve of, it is likely that I will get what I really mean. But you can't tell me what sort of wish that is."

"Just so," she said, the slightest frown appearing briefly on her face. I saw something I wasn't sure I understood there in her eyes. It's a nerd thing... we aren't good with social signals, you know?

Then I had an idea. "My first wish," I said. "I wish that, whenever I look at someone just so," and I squinted just a bit at her, "I would then know the desires of the person I am looking at."

She smiled. "As you wish, so shall it be."

Wasting no time, I immediately squinted *just so* at her, and I knew her heart's desire. But as soon as I did, I realized I didn't yet know all that I needed to know. I thought about the situation carefully for a few moments, and she waited patiently.

"Interesting," I said at last. "Tell me, if you are allowed to, how you came to be imprisoned in that bottle."

"I was a princess," she said. "I received the bottle as a gift from one who did not know what it contained; I'm sure he stole it. I opened it, and the djinn inside offered me three wishes. I was not so careful as you when I made them. First I wished to be beautiful, for though I was high born I was not very attractive, and he made me so. Then I wished a great prince would fall in love with me and worship at my feet, and he made that so also. At last, overcome with the sort of desire that only one whose every wish has been granted can feel, I wished for the power to do the things the djinn could do."

She paused, and I said, "So he traded places with you, making you the djinn of the bottle and slave to anyone who opened it."

"Just so," she said, looking down. "The prince who had worshiped at my feet had great sport with me then, and the former djinn became his vizier. When the prince, guided by his vizier so I could not twist his words, had exhausted the three wishes I could grant him, he ordered that the bottle be sealed and buried in the furthest part of his kingdom in a place where no one would ever think to look for it. I have been within the bottle awaiting release ever since."

Her story agreed very closely with the desires I had seen when I squinted at her. I said, "You have been imprisoned for a long time. I've read stories about djinns trapped in bottles... they say that some of them go mad."

"I did," she said. "I spent a long time, perhaps a thousand years, planning the wondrous things I would do for whomever freed me; and another thousand years planning the horrible retribution I would mete out to that person. But that is all past me now, and I am resigned to my fate."

I thought then that I should have asked her those questions before making my first wish... but then, how would I have been sure she was telling me the truth?

"I have learned almost all that I want to know now," I said. "Can you tell me about how the bottle was created and the first djinn trapped inside?"

"I don't know that," she said. "But you could wish to know."

"I could," I said, thinking. I had already made a wish that allowed her into my head, so to speak; I didn't want to risk another like that. I smiled as the answer came to me. "I wish that you knew and would tell me the history of the bottle and of those who inhabited it before you."

She smiled again. "You are a careful man," she said. "The djinn who came before me was the first to be trapped within the bottle. He had been a mighty king, but like many great kings he wished for even more power. His vizier told him of the djinni, those made of smokeless flame who wield great power, and the king ordered the vizier to find a way to entrap one and compel it to serve him. The vizier communed with powers in worlds other than this and learned how to create the bottle and how to summon a djinn, but those he communed with did not tell him the whole truth. So it happened that, when the djinn stood before the king and the king, holding the bottle, ordered the djinn into it, he spoke wrongly. The great djinn, laughing, transformed the king into a djinn and trapped him in the bottle instead. The king was then commanded by his own son, his heir, and thereafter the bottle changed hands many times before being stolen by the one who gave it to me."

"I see," I said. "I think I understand. The king wanted power, and he got it only at the cost of his freedom. The great djinn gave him power he could never use for his own purposes. He was only freed when you wished for the power, and by giving it to you he trapped you the same way."

"Yes," she said, with equal parts anger and sadness in her voice, or so it seemed to me.

I squinted at her again... took a second look, just to be sure. I had just one wish left, and the temptation to use it to make myself rich or powerful was strong, but I knew practically from the start that I could never pull off such a wish without her turning it against me. No, I had to align my wish with her desires or it would all go wrong.

I sighed, thinking for one last time of the endless riches I might have asked for. Then I said, "I wish that the power you possess would return to the great djinn from whom it came."

"As you wish, so shall it be," she said, rather quickly. Just like that, the bottle crumbled to fine sand and ran through my fingers, and a sort of a wave of faint light passed over her body. She smiled at me again. "I'm free," she said. "At last, after so long, I'm free!"

"I'm glad," I said, and really, I was glad for her.

"My name is Jamilah," she said. "It has been a very long time since I told that to anyone. A very long time since I was allowed to do so."

"I'm Rob," I said, holding out my hand. She took it, awkwardly, and I held her hand gently as I spoke to her. "What will you do now?"

"I do not know," she said. "I know nothing of what has become of the world in the many years I was trapped within the bottle. I will need a guide and protector." She looked into my eyes, meaningfully.

"Of course," I said. I decided that damned ugly pot could wait until tomorrow. Guiding her by the hand to the battered Land Rover I had rented, I said, "Princess, come with me, and I'll introduce you to the wonders of the modern world. Starting with air conditioning and indoor plumbing."

She smiled at me with a mixture of happiness and puzzlement, and I knew that in the end I had made all the right wishes. Oh, it might be like a rebound relationship, where she only thought she loved me as long as she needed me, but I decided I'd take that risk.

After all, even if she left me in the end, the whole thing wouldn't be a total loss... a quick squint at her when she wasn't looking revealed that at least one wish had not gone to waste after all.

Clandestine Delivery

Captain Cross laid down his sextant and scope, and absently stroked the burnished wood of the helm. The bridge was dark and quiet; the Captain couldn't help but savor that strange peace. The bridge, after all, was rarely empty.

His was a foolish plan, and he knew it... that's why he threw a party back at Cristobel. He told his officers and crew that he had found them a new commission, one which would pay them all handsomely. Only two men were left to guard the ship, while everyone else ate, drank, and made merry.

It was a simple matter for Cross to slip away from the party. The guards were surprised to see him back so soon. "At ease, boys," he told them. "I've got a bottle of unusually fine rum in my quarters which I've come back to retrieve." They sat down, resuming the card game he had interrupted; so they were unprepared for the tranquilizer darts he shot them with a moment later.

Cross had been worried that he might be seen on the dock, dragging the two men from his ship, but it was late and he was lucky. A few minutes later the Raging Moon moved slowly out of port.

"Well," the Captain said to the empty bridge, "I'm wasting time. Let's be on our way!" He tried to brace himself mentally, as he always did, and pushed forward the polished wooden lever. For a moment there was almost total darkness, the stars gone... the only light he could see was that soft glow illuminating the instruments of the bridge stations.

Then the sky was ablaze! The sky was filled with countless brilliant stars, many large enough to show as small disks; and arrayed in front of the ship, impossibly large, were the Sun, Mercury, Venus, Earth, and Mars. Turning, the Captain saw Jupiter looming large behind him. At length the Captain drew a breath... "Damn," he said, "I'll never get used to that."

His course was already calculated, so there was nothing else to do but open the solar sails and get under way. At the helm, he pushed forward another lever, and watched through the ironglass dome as the five giant sails folded out radially from the long mast. It stretched out before the ship, sails of optical diode fabric, transparent from the front but mirrored on the back. The extended sails glowed with a brilliant double image of the fiery sky, and like the seed of a dandelion the ship moved forward, carried by the solar wind.

"This is why I went to space," he said to no one. Standing at the helm station, he basked in the filtered light of a thousand suns. The ship moved in stately fashion past the planets and the Sun, slowly accelerating.

As the ship moved beyond the gravity well of Sol, the hyperdrive's Porter-Sung radius increased; even as the planets fell behind the stars seemed to come closer. Captain Cross piloted his ship in bright silence for what seemed a long time.

At length the ship passed beyond the orbit of Pluto, and he knew it was time. Cross arose from the helm station, picked up his sextant and scope and took sightings for the first course correction.

The recalculations completed, he sat at the navigator's station idly stroking the elegant wood-clad calculator his father had given him. He could still remember that day, nine years earlier, as if it were yesterday; he had just graduated with honors from the Admiralty's Fleet Academy, and received his navigator's license. It was May the first, 2244, and the fall weather in Sydney was clear, breezy, and beautiful. His future seemed bright indeed.

That day was also his birthday. "You're charmed, Nate," his father had said. "Graduating on your birthday must be worth something, after all."

A strange noise made Cross leap to his feet. Turning, he saw a slender woman framed by the bridge hatch. "Kat," he said sternly. "What are you doing here?"

"What are you doing, Captain? Why have you left the crew behind?"

"None of your business, Ensign," he said as gruffly as he could manage. "Why aren't you back on Cristobel with the rest of the crew?"

She shrugged. "Didn't feel like partying," she said. "Stayed in the bunkroom, fell asleep."

"And how long have you been back there, spying on me?" he asked.

"A while." She walked more fully onto the bridge. The Captain realized then how little he knew about Katherine DeAngelis, his new Helm Officer. She had replaced Tony Gannon after he got himself killed on Europa. All he really knew about her was that she was a fine pilot, and as tightly self-controlled as the braid in her long dark hair.

"Well, you're here," he said. "Can I count on you?"

"Of course, Captain," she answered. "If you'll say what's going on?"

"I have a course correction to make," he said, reaching for the paper he'd written the figures on. Kat took it from his hand.

"Helm Officer's job, sir," she said, moving to the helm station.

"Your insolence isn't becoming an officer on my ship," he said smiling.

"On a pirate ship, sir?" she said, gently manipulating the controls. "Thought it was a job requirement."

Later they prepared a cold lunch of crackers, cheese, hard sausage and dried fruit. "Tea, Captain?" asked Kat, as she poured herself a glass of the strong cold drink.

"No, Ensign, I believe I'll have the red wine."

"Alcohol, sir?" she said, frowning. "With only two officers on duty?"

"Just a glass, Ensign. You needn't worry about your Captain getting soused." There was a time, he remembered, when he would have agreed with her admonition... but times had changed and so had he.

They sat down together at the Captain's table. "So what about the mission, sir?"

Between mouthfuls he told her. "Remember that courier ship we found last week?"

"With a hole in her sail, dome shattered, pilots missing?" she replied.

"Yeah," he said. "Drake and I went through the contents... mail and packages mostly. I happened to see this." Cross pulled a small flat box from his jacket and offered it to her.

She looked at the address:

> Captain Nathaniel Cross
> Slip 21, Lower Ring
> Cristobel Station
> Sol

"Addressed to you?" she stated more than asked. "Strange. No return either."

Cross opened the box, offering Kat the vid-disc inside. There was a large vid screen there in the mess, spoils of an old score; she put the disc into the slot. Momentarily the screen lit up, displaying the head and shoulders of a beautiful woman.

"Captain Cross," the image said, "we hope this message finds you doing well. I represent a small but wealthy colony which has need of your services. We will pay you five hundred thousand Martian Dominion dollars for a single courier run, and we will pay you ten percent as a show of good faith. When you arrive at our location we will pay you that sum immediately."

"Wow," said Kat quietly as the woman on the screen paused.

"We don't expect this to be a particularly dangerous mission, but your discretion is paramount. Tell no one about this message. It might be best if you left your crew behind this time." The screen cleared, and then a star chart was displayed. Kat stood up to look at it closer.

"Twenty light-years in the general direction of Aldebaran," she said. "Nothing out there I can think of."

"No habitable worlds, if that's what you mean. I assume it's a mining colony of some sort. I've no idea what I'm to be transporting, but it must be important to them."

"D'ya believe that part about the mission not being dangerous?" she asked.

"I'm not sure. I'm risking playing it her way because of all the money."

"Greed before a fall, eh?" she replied.

"Perhaps."

"Word is, you were Admiralty," she said, changing the subject. "True?"

"True," he answered. "I was a Lieutenant, Second Navigator aboard the Valiant."

"She's a tough ship, I hear."

"Yes. I think Captain Ragan is still in command... she's the best captain in the Fleet. I'd hate to face the Valiant now." Cross took a sip from his glass. "Anyway, I was on leave. I went to Sydney, to see my fiancé Mariel. I had good news for her, and I had a mind to surprise her. My surprise... she was away visiting a cousin and wouldn't be back until the next day."

"So what'd you do?" Kat asked.

"What else? I hit the bars. I drank slow, paced myself... planned to make a night of it. I don't even remember how it started, but suddenly this drunk in civvies was yelling at me. I tried to talk to him, offered him a drink, but he just got more belligerent. Next thing I knew he'd drawn a knife."

"Bad situation," Kat said as the Captain paused for another sip. "Since you're here, suppose he didn't do so well."

"Nope. There was a struggle, and I didn't plan it that way, but he took the blade in the belly. I'd been in a couple of battles before, but he's the first man I ever killed who I saw die. I just stood there over him staring... had the knife in my hand. Then I heard someone say, 'that man just murdered Randy Johnson! Pulled a knife on him, he did!' I was about to tell him how he was wrong when the bartender leaned over the bar and said, 'Son, that's Admiral Johnson's grandson. You better run now, and don't slow down.'"

"Johnson? The Admiral from Texas?" she said, shaking her head. "Took the bartender's advice then, Captain?"

"I did. I had rented a car, but I couldn't remember if anyone inside had heard my name... so I took off on foot instead. Around the corner was a drunk getting into a car with Fleet plates on it. He was too drunk to be driving anyway, so I ran up and said something like, 'Hey, friend, headed back to base? Let me drive you.' He cooperated, which was a mercy for me. I put him in the back seat, and he fell over and went to sleep; the gate guard waved me right through."

Kat was leaning closer over the Captain's table as he finished his wine, her green almond-shaped eyes shining with interest. Cross wondered for the thousandth time what she had against personal pronouns, which she seemed to use only when forced to, but Drake had warned him not to ask her too many questions if he wanted to keep her aboard...

"Anyway... remember I told you I had good news for Mariel?" Kat nodded. "I had been promising her for three years that I would resign my commission when I saved enough to buy a small trader's ship. She worried about me dying in the line of duty... that was in '49, and there were still occasional skirmishes with your people."

"My people?" Kat said, a bit hotly. "A Martian, you're thinking? Not so."

Cross was confused then. Katherine DeAngelis was tall and very slim, with the slightly enlarged ribcage which was the result of ancestral genetic engineering. Even her medium-brown skin and almond eyes marked her as a Martian.

Don't ask questions, he thought, then gave in and did it anyway. "If you're not Martian, then what are you?"

"Born in space, raised on Cristobel. Never set foot on Mars." She sat back and crossed her arms, smugly.

"I see," he said. "Anyway, I'd had the money for more than a year, and just hadn't been able to... you know, do it. Take that step. But then I heard about a ship for sale on New Britannia Station. I bought it, just before I came down to Earth. Paid cash, but I hadn't filed the new registry papers yet... so there was no record that it was mine. All I had to do was get back up to New Britannia."

"You stole a launch?"

"Yup. I realized that, if they figured out who I was, they'd be watching the base for me, and the civilian spaceport also. But there was one place I figured, at that time of night, they wouldn't be on guard... Fleet Academy."

"Stole a trainer?"

"Better than that. I stole the Admiral's Gig. I knew that Admiral O'Malley, chief of the Academy, always had the fastest launch they could build him. I also knew the security there was lax... I didn't even have to fight anyone to take it. By the time they realized that it wasn't the Admiral flying his Gig, I was already aboard the Dora Dell."

"This ship?"

"Yup. I went straight to Mars, checked in at Phobos, and got my privateer's license right away. I can't say I enjoyed that period, but I guess I'm good at surviving. My recent knowledge of Fleet operations made me an instant success in the privateer business, and Drake and Logan joined me right away. It took a while to get a really good crew together though..."

"Changed her name to Raging Moon. Why?"

"Dora Dell didn't sound very warlike, and my first stop was Phobos, so the name seemed appropriate. Heard it in a classical song once." Cross got up to refill his glass. "Went pretty well for about a year and a half, then the Martian Senate decided to normalize diplomatic relations with Earth. That meant that Earth criminals hiding out on Mars would be extradited. Most of the privateer captains said it'd never happen, but I had my slip on Cristobel rented a week in advance. We've been freelancers since then."

"Proper pirates, you mean."

Cross nodded. "Well, time to check our course. Since you're with me, I'll take the first night watch and you can have the second."

"How were you going to handle it alone?" she asked.

"Sleep on the deck on the bridge, with the hyperdrive detector tapped into the intercom speakers instead of the signals headset. Rage doesn't need babysitting on a deep-space journey. Given a choice, I'd rather sleep in my bunk."

On the bridge, Captain Cross took the required sightings. "Not off course enough to be worth adjusting," he mused.

"How long is a night shift for two?" Kat asked.

"I'll give you six hours this time," he replied. "I've been up quite a while already. You'll give me the same, then we're both up for six hours, then we change to eight hour shifts at that point."

"Yes, sir," she said, turning to leave. "What's that noise?"

He listened, and the sound got louder. "The hyperdrive detector!" They moved in unison to the signals station. Cross quickly studied the instruments. "Two ships, big ones... only the Admiralty has such large ships. They're headed Earthward on an opposite vector... no, they're changing course toward us!"

"Raging Moon is no match for them, sir, even with full crew!" Kat said.

"Never fear, Ensign," the Captain replied. "They'll never find us." He moved to the helm station, taking Kat's regular seat, and reached under the console.

The stars went out, plunging the ship into total darkness. Only the faint light of the instruments remained.

"What happened?" Kat asked.

"I disengaged the phase oscillator... we are completely in hyperspace. The sails are useless now," and he pulled back the lever, closing them, "but the fusion rockets are still effective." Cross flipped the switches for the three fusion drive rockets, then pushed their trio of throttles forward slowly. "In an hour or so I'll turn the oscillator back on and resume sailing."

"Won't they still detect our hyperdrive, sir?" the young Ensign asked.

"No. The hyperdrive detector doesn't detect a hyperdrive... that's just what you are supposed to think. It detects energy leaked when the Porter-Sung radius of two or more imbalanced hyperdrives come in contact, and the entire P-S effect is caused by the oscillator. It keeps us just less than point oh oh one out of phase. Only senior Helm and Engineering personnel are told that, in the Admiralty at least."

"How did you find out?"

"Drunken engineer. Alcohol has taught me much. So anyway, the first thing I did to convert Dora Dell into Raging Moon was rig a button under the helm console to a relay which disengages the oscillator."

"Were you ever going to teach your new Helm Officer?" she asked, hands on hips.

"When she needed to know. Consider yourself taught. Now off to your bunk, Ensign! You're on duty in six hours."

"Aye, sir," she said as she walked out. Cross put his boots up on the edge of the helm station to wait.

An hour or so later, the Captain shut down the fusion rockets, reactivated the oscillator and resumed sailing. Only a few minutes passed before he heard the hyperdrive detector again.

"Damn," he said, looking at the scope at the signals station. "Same two... guess I'll just have to try harder." Resuming his seat at the helm, Cross changed course by eye toward a star chosen at random, near his previous course. He let the pursuers close halfway before he pushed the button under the console.

Plunged once again into darkness, Captain Cross switched over to fusion rockets once again, rotated the ship to a random orientation, then pulled the ship's nose up ninety degrees. "That ought to keep them out of my hair," he said to no one.

Again he let an hour pass, and this time the pursuing ships were gone when he resumed sailing. It took him a few minutes with the sextant and scope to figure out where the Raging Moon now was, and a few minutes more to assume a corrected course.

Cross awoke with a start... he'd dozed off in the helm station chair, feet up on the console. "Damn," he cursed under his breath. The chronometer said he'd been asleep six hours... so Kat had received her eight hours after all.

He quickly checked the ship's course, then left the bridge. It was a short trip up the port zero-G ladder tube to the officer's bunkroom. The hatch stood slightly ajar, and he made a mental note to reprimand Kat for it. Then he saw her, through the half-open hatch.

She was sitting on her bunk, rebraiding her hair. He had heard that she did so every morning, but he'd never seen it. Her hands moved, working behind her head, with such swiftness and surety that he could hardly believe it. This was obviously what made her such a fine Helm Officer.

He watched her finish the braid with an elastic band. Then she turned and looked directly at him, quizzically. "Up and at 'em," he said, embarrassed to be caught watching her. His Admiralty training permitted no fraternization with subordinate officers or crew, and even after becoming a full-fledged pirate, he still held to those ideals.

"Any trouble, Captain?" she said, rising to her feet and straightening her uniform.

"The Admiralty ships were still behind us when I resumed course, so I took Rage back under, made a random jog sideways, then recalculated our course. I think I lost them this time, but keep a weather eye out."

"Aye," she said.

When Cross had slept, he joined his ensign on the bridge for a meal, and they began a chess game which they played through the remainder of their voyage. Far off the main travel corridors, they expected no encounters, and they had none.

Cross tried several times to draw Kat out in conversation, but the ensign deflected all his personal queries. Her evasion only made him more curious... but then he realized his interest was beginning to be more than just the interest of a Captain in his crew. It was something he couldn't allow in himself.

Finally the star which was their destination loomed large in front of the ship, and Captain Cross ordered, "Retract sails and disengage hyperdrive."

"Aye, Captain," she said, first drawing in the sails, then as they folded back against the mast she threw the lever to turn off the hyperdrive. In an instant, the normal blackness of space sprinkled with pinpoint stars was restored. The red dwarf they were approaching seemed to move away also, becoming no larger in the sky than the Moon seen from Earth, and about as bright through the light-filtering dome over the bridge.

"Check mass detector," he said, as he lifted his binoculars and began scanning the skies.

"One Neptune-class planet, twenty-two mark fourteen, plus several dwarf planets, none of them close. The large planet seems to have several moons." Cross turned his binoculars toward the planet and quickly located it; livid red and orange clouds made an angry pattern of streaks on the face of it.

It was then that Cross heard the beeping from the unmanned comm station. "It's a beacon," he said. "Coming from the large planet. Line up on it, helm, and engage hyperdrive." As Kat threw the lever, the planet and star both seemed to leap forward, with the planet slightly closer, or so it appeared. "Fusion thrusters, advance slowly, let's see what's here."

Cross scanned the planet with his binoculars, and shortly saw a shining spot in the clouds... a gas mining platform, easily identified by the distinctive shape of its great gas-collecting sails. "Let's get within a light-second so we can communicate."

A few moments later, after consulting the mass detector and working a few moments with his calculator, Cross said, "That's good, let's stop here," and Kat disengaged the thrusters and hyperdrive simultaneously.

They were close enough to the planet that it didn't appear to leap away, but just shrank a bit as she did so. Checking the comm console, he said, "We're being hailed," then picked up the microphone and flipped a switch. "This is Captain Cross of the Raging Moon. I received your message and am here to pick up your cargo."

What he heard next chilled him to the bone. "Captain Cross, welcome to Mining Platform Gamma Twelve," said a clearly robotic voice.

Cross turned to the ensign and ordered, "Sails out, hard about and engage," but even as he gave the order he saw her hand already throwing the lever to open the sails.

"Wait, Captain," came the mechanical voice. "We mean you no harm. Please hold for our envoy."

Then a different voice came over the wireless. "Captain Cross, please don't leave." It was a woman's voice.

Cross held up his hand, and Kat paused with her hand on the hyperdrive lever. She said, "Captain, it's a trap. Let me throw the switch and we're out of here."

"Captain, please answer me," came the plaintive voice of the woman, scratchy over the wireless.

"Hold a moment, but don't let go of that lever," he said to Kat. Then he said into the microphone, "This is Captain Cross. Please identify yourself."

"Rebecca Holden, of Earth," she replied.

"Rebecca," he said, sweating from the tension of being so close to a robot enclave, "what are you doing here?"

"I'm trapped," she replied. "My ship was wrecked near here ten years ago."

"What ship was that?" he asked.

"HMS Dayton," she replied. "I'm the only survivor."

Cross keyed off his microphone. "The Dayton," he said to Kat.

"The best-known lost ship of the space era," she replied. "I remember when it was on the news. Left Thirty-nine Tauri A Four bound for Earth but never arrived."

"Captain, are you there?" came Rebecca's voice. "They tell me to have you check at two ninety three mark two."

Cross raised his binoculars again and checked the heading. "Damn, that's the Dayton," he said. "In orbit. Half the mast is smashed, and the forecabin is extensively damaged, but the name is clearly visible."

"This star system is more than five light years off the approved course to Sol from Thirty-nine Tauri," said Kat.

"Whatever they hit must have thrown them off course," the Captain replied. Keying the microphone, he said, "Rebecca, the Dayton is a wreck. How did you survive?"

"My mom put me in my spacesuit after the crash," she said. "Our cabin wasn't damaged too badly, but the air was leaking out. She put her spacesuit on too, but it had a leak. She died holding me." Cross could hear the sadness in her voice, and it moved him. But he was still suspicious.

"How do I know this isn't a trap?"

"I promise it isn't," she said. "These robots are nice, not like the ones that tried to take over the Earth. They live on this old mining platform, and try to stay away from humans. They don't want to fight, really. When they found the Dayton drifting, they brought it to the planet. They rescued me."

Cross looked at his ensign, and saw that she was frowning, hand still poised to throw the ship into hyperspace. "Rebecca, I'm sorry to have to ask this, but how can I be sure this isn't a trap?"

"The robots said you'd say that, and it's okay. I'll come over in a small launch, and stop a kilometer away, then cross in a spacesuit, and you can check all my gear and throw out anything that worries you. I don't have anything I can't leave behind."

Kat mouthed the word "Payment" to Cross, and he nodded at her. "That sounds good enough, Rebecca, but I have to ask how the robots intend to pay us. I can't just take you on out of the goodness of my heart."

"I know, Captain," she said, and he could hear the smile in her voice, which was low and musical. "They told me to tell you that they can't actually pay you in

Dominion dollars, but they want to offer you a hundred kilograms of ruthenium, which they say is valuable."

Cross drew a surprised breath... ruthenium, a key component in hyperdrive inductors, was one of the most valuable metals in existence. "All up front, nothing held until we get back to Sol?"

"Yes," she answered. "Please, Captain, I know you're suspicious. The robots are hoping to establish relations with Earth. They kept me here, it's true, but they were kind to me, as much as robots can be. The robots here are programmed for science. All they want to do is study the universe. They use the mining platform as a research facility, but they also keep the mine running, which is how they have the ruthenium. Their hope is that, by sending me to Earth unharmed, they'll convince at least a few humans that trading materials and scientific data with them is a good idea."

"I see... you're a peace offering," Cross replied.

"Exactly."

Cross keyed off the microphone. "Ensign DeAngelis, I'm going to agree to their offer."

"But, sir, it's a trap! It has to be," she replied.

"It might be. Which is why I'll be standing there with my hand on the hyperdrive while you let her in the airlock with our ruthenium. Put on your space suit, take the robot scanner and check the ruthenium. Throw out everything else she brings except the clothes she is wearing, and scan them just in case. Hell, search her. Once you're sure she's not carrying any technology, buzz me and we'll get out of here."

Captain Cross could tell DeAngelis wasn't happy about the situation, but she said, "Aye, Captain," somewhat reluctantly and left the bridge.

Kat stood in the open airlock waiting for the girl to make the crossing. The ensign's spacesuit was black with cat's eye logos painted on the shoulders for identification. Kat could see the launch, almost exactly a kilometer away and perfectly synchronized with the Raging Moon, and she easily saw the moment when the girl came out of it. She was wearing a plain white spacesuit, and piloting a small cargo sled which Kat could see was loaded with a pile of something under a silver tarp.

When the girl and the sled reached the airlock, Kat could see the girl's face through her helmet visor, and was shocked to realize it was the woman on the vid disc. She was blonde and pretty, perhaps twenty years old, and smiling nervously. Kat did a cursory scan with the robot detector; when it showed green, she said, "Rebecca, welcome aboard," without any particular enthusiasm.

"Thank you," replied the girl, pulling herself into the airlock. "The ruthenium is on the cargo sled. Let me help you bring it in."

Kat applied the robot detector to the sled-load of metal before allowing Rebecca to touch any of it. Together they unloaded the small, heavy ingots of gray metal from the sled into a crate. It was easy work in the zero gravity of the airlock. Once the ingots were transferred, Kat gave the sled a firm kick away from the hatch and shot it repeatedly with her blaster, eliciting a squeal from Rebecca.

She admired the faintly-glowing wreckage of the sled for a moment, then closed the hatch and pressurized the airlock. "Strip," she said, pointing her blaster at Rebecca. For a moment, Kat thought the girl would protest, but instead she silently complied, and shortly Rebecca stood naked before the ensign. She smiled nervously as Kat passed the robot detection bar up and down her body; in the cool air of the airlock, she had goosebumps over much of her skin.

Finally Kat said, "Okay, get dressed, but don't touch the space suit."

"Yes, Ma'am," replied the girl, dressing as quickly as she could. She had plain gray slacks, a gray pullover shirt, and a pair of soft gray slippers, all apparently of the same material. Kat considered commenting that she could get some nicer things after they got back to Sol, but her distrust kept her silent.

As soon as the space suit had been ejected, Kat pushed the intercom button on the wall beside the airlock. "We're go, Captain," and instantly she felt the ship lurch slightly.

On the bridge, Kat took her place at the helm. "Rebecca, welcome aboard," said Captain Cross, holding out his hand.

Rebecca took his hand gracefully. "Thank you, Captain."

"Nathaniel," he said. "Nathaniel Cross, Captain of the Raging Moon."

"Pleased to meet you, Nathaniel." She looked out at the blazing stars that seemed to be crowding the ship. "I love to see that," she said. "I was just twelve when I got aboard the Dayton with my mother, and I just sat and looked out our cabin window most of the time."

She had not withdrawn her hand, and Cross glanced down at it. Her hand was warm and dry, with soft skin and well-maintained nails. Then he met her gaze and realized she had noticed his attention... she had a small, shy smile on her face, and was very slightly blushing. "I need to plot a course to Sol," he said quickly, and he guided her to the navigator's table and pulled out the extra seat provided for the navigator's mate. "Please, have a seat while I work."

Cross picked up his sextant, located appropriate guide stars from memory, and made notes on their positions; consulting his thick, dog-eared copy of Quincy's Navigational Ephemeris and his calculator, he quickly worked out a correct heading direct to Sol, and when he had it, he called the numbers out to Ensign DeAngelis. "Take a half shift at the helm, and then we'll arrange something to eat and switch shifts when we're done."

"Aye, Captain," replied the ensign.

"Would you like to see our ship?" he said, turning to Rebecca.

"Oh, yes," she replied. "That would be wonderful."

Over the next several days, Rebecca spent most of her time with the captain. It seemed obvious that Kat didn't like her, a fact which did not escape Cross, but there was little he could do so long as the ensign was at least civil to the girl, and she always was.

"We're a few days from Sol now," he said to Rebecca as he stood at the helm station one day. "Are you looking forward to being there?"

"I am," she said. "If nothing has happened to them, I should still have an uncle, two aunts, and maybe my grandparents as well. They seemed really old when I was shipwrecked, but I was just twelve, and everyone older than my mother just had to be ancient, you know?"

Cross laughed with her. "I know," he said. "Strange how things change as you get a little older."

"Lots of things change when you get a little older, Nathaniel," she said, and Cross thought he saw something in her eyes he hadn't seen before... a fire he hadn't seen in a woman's eyes since he became a pirate, for he wouldn't partake of the women for hire at Cristobel, and he wouldn't fraternize with any of the women of his crew. He felt a complementary fire begin in himself, a feeling he had been avoiding for days but which he realized had always been there.

He was about to make some awkward reply when Ensign DeAngelis arrived on the bridge. "I'm here to relieve you, Captain," she said.

"Very good, Ensign," he said, stepping aside for her.

As the ensign took her station, Rebecca leaned close to the Captain, sliding her hand around his bicep, and whispered, "Show me your cabin?"

Rather than answer, he just nodded and led the way. Rebecca slid her hand down to take his, and followed behind him in the narrow corridors of the ship.

His cabin was the largest on the ship, but it was by no means large. It had room for a decent sized bunk, a wide locker, and a small desk, all securely bolted to the deck. Rebecca slipped past him into the room and sat down on the bed. "Nice," she said. "Join me?"

"Rebecca," he replied, "this is probably not a good idea. You haven't had human contact in what, ten years? You probably think you're in love with me. Remember, I'm a pirate captain who took you aboard for money, not a knight in shining armor riding in to save you for our happily-ever-after."

She smiled broadly at him. "I know," she said. "I've watched television shows, and read books. I'm not in love with you, and I know you're not in love with me.

I have no illusions about any of it. But you're a man, a good looking man, even an honorable man for a pirate. You're the first man I've seen since I was old enough to know that I like men, and I think you like me too." She stood up then and put her hands on his hips. "I've never been with a man. I want you to be first."

She leaned in, eyes closed, head tipped back for a kiss, and after the briefest delay Cross kissed her. He could tell she had never been kissed before, but she was a quick learner. Then she took his hand and placed it on her breast, and Cross gave in to his feelings at last.

They got undressed quickly; her clothing came off easier than his did, and she laughed happily as she worked out how to get his pants undone while he took off his shirt. When he was finally naked, she lay back on his bed and stretched out her arms toward him, and he went willingly into them and buried his face in her hair, kissing her ear and listening to her moan with pleasure.

"Damn," he said, "I almost forgot. You surely aren't on any sort of birth control, are you?" She shook her head, and he disengaged himself from her and stood up. "I've got condoms in my locker," he said, taking the mere two steps needed to reach it. Reaching inside, he found what he was looking for and turned back, saying, "Here it is."

Rebecca was airborne, arms outstretched and fingers hooked like claws, with the strangest blank expression on her face. Nathaniel Cross opened fire with the blaster in his hand, shooting her once in the abdomen and once between her beautiful breasts. The force of the plasma blasts threw her backward onto the bed.

He stepped carefully forward, staying out of range of her spasmodically clutching right hand. The smell of burnt plastic filled the air, and Cross could see the half-melted mechanisms inside her ruptured torso. He looked straight into her blue eyes and saw sadness. "How did you know?" she asked him.

He answered her by firing a round into her face.

The door burst open and Kat rushed in, saying "Heard blaster fire... are you alright, Captain?"

"Yes, Ensign," he said. She saw that he seemed entirely unashamed of his nudity, but his face was unreadable, too full of conflicting emotions for her to follow. "We'll need to clean this up. Are we still in hyperspace?"

"No, sir. Dropped out as soon as shots sounded. Assumed you didn't want the ship flying blind."

"Very good. You were right, you know... this was a trap." He sighed, then continued, "I suppose I'll need to get dressed so we can clean this up."

"Pardon, Captain... how did you know?"

"Not now," he replied, pulling on his discarded pants. "Not until this... thing is off my ship. It might contain some recording device, maybe even a transmitter of some sort. I won't give them any advantage if I can avoid it."

They ejected the burned carcass of the machine who had been Rebecca from the airlock, along with her clothing, then spent several hours in the ship's mechanical shop breaking all the ruthenium ingots in half to look for hidden devices. When they determined there were no unexplained devices of any sort on the ship, Kat said, "Leaving now, sir?"

"Not quite yet. We each have one more task. Get an emergency beacon and put it out with the robot, then meet me on the bridge."

"Why, sir?"

"The Admiralty needs to know about this. They may be able to get some intelligence from the robot's carcass. So I'm going to go get a fix on our location, and when we get back to Cristobel I'll send them a message."

"Ah. So the beacon is to help find it."

"Exactly. Now look sharp! I want to be underway shortly."

The Captain had his fix plotted by the time DeAngelis arrived at the bridge. "Resume our previous course, Lieutenant DeAngelis."

Kat had the ship in hyperspace and underway before she realized what he had said. "Lieutenant, sir?"

"Any time an ensign proves smarter than the Captain, that ensign should either be promoted or launched out the airlock."

"Ah... thank you, sir," she said, smiling nervously. "Glad you chose to promote."

"Promote you, hell," he said, trying to look serious but failing badly. "I'm glad I hired you."

"Sir, perhaps your Helm Officer isn't that smart." she said. "Still can't figure out how you knew she was a robot."

He looked at Kat for a moment, considering his words. Finally he said, "She didn't smell right. She looked, and sounded, and felt entirely human. Every detail was right, down to the pores and fine hairs on her skin. But when I got close to her... hell, when I was kissing her ear, so I had my nose in her hair, I realized she didn't smell at all. Humans always have a smell, be it good or bad, but she didn't smell like anything."

"Never considered that," she replied.

"Neither did the robots who designed her. Good thing for us, eh?"

"Yes, sir," she said, smiling grimly. "It means we have a chance."

Time Lost

It all began with a headache.

I was sitting in my office, at my desk, looking over reports, when it hit me. It was blinding at first. I think I cried out. After a few moments it faded a bit, and I got up and stumbled out into the hallway.

Everyone was still, frozen. For a moment I stood still also.

My head still hurt, a lot. But everything looked so strange. I walked down the hallway; there was Tim from Accounting, talking to some young intern I didn't recognize. It was a frozen moment, like a photograph, with her looking down the hallway, apparently distracted, mouth open in mid-word; he was frozen in the act of looking at her cleavage. I laughed, feeling a bit dizzy, and it sounded somehow muffled.

A few steps further and I saw Rob, my co-worker, at his desk; he was leaning over, and I could see he was looking at that intern's legs. Nobody would have seen him, normally. I laughed again, and my head throbbed.

There's a fountain, a sort of waterfall, near the elevators opposite the reception desk. It was frozen also. I looked at it in wonder, then reached out to touch it. It was hard and cold.

And then it was wet. My head stopped hurting so suddenly that it felt ten pounds lighter. The water was rushing over my hand, getting my sleeve wet. I drew back and looked around.

The receptionist was looking at me strangely, but nobody else seemed to have noticed. I walked back to my office quickly; Tim was still talking with the intern, and Rob was studiously ignoring them. I smiled as I walked by.

What had happened? At first I thought I was imagining it... some sort of migraine-induced hallucination, though you know I'd never had a migraine before. I didn't get any more work done that day... I was too busy trying to understand.

By the time the week had passed it had happened three more times, and I couldn't help but believe it. Each time lasted a bit longer, and each time the pain was less.

Then came the night that I got up to use the bathroom, and walked through the door. No, really *through the door...* I was intangible. There was no headache this time, and for a few moments I just sort of drifted through the walls; I couldn't touch the floor anymore, so I couldn't walk. I focused my mind on the situation, and then the headache started... but after a few moments, I fell back into the world. Literally fell, three or four inches that I had drifted upward off that last step.

Things were different from that moment on. I gained control over my newfound powers. I could stop time whenever I felt like it, and I could walk through walls, and my head hardly hurt anymore. I learned to slow time, rather than stopping it, and to speed it up; when I tried to run time backward, though, I hit a head-splitting wall.

I'm embarrassed to admit that it took me a while to realize that I needed to be intangible to run time backward. I was literally running into myself.

Once I did it, time was wide open for me. I could travel forward or back, fast or slow, and apparently I was also invisible and inaudible when I was intangible. I couldn't hear anyone else while I was that way, either, but I could still see, though things were a bit dimmer when I did it.

I didn't tell anyone about my powers. I could prove it, now, but I knew I couldn't continue my comfortable life if too many people found out, and I didn't feel ready yet.

One morning as I stood ready to leave for work, I felt the beginnings of another headache. Though I reveled in my new powers, I was worried about the headaches... I had begun to suspect something serious was wrong with me.

I drove to the library, instead of going to work. I went forward a decade at a time, using the computers and books of the library to track the advancement of technology. After seventy years, things finally looked right.

I stole the robot from the factory. He was an off-the-shelf medical robot, meant for service in the Third World; I watched over the shoulder of the technician, noting his access codes, so when the robot "awoke" it already considered me its master.

I took the stolen robot to a hotel room, in what I still thought of as the present. I didn't bother to actually rent one, I just made sure the one I used would be empty all day.

"Good afternoon, sir," it said as it booted up. "How can I be of service?"

"First, I need you to perform a diagnostic on me. I do not want you to make any changes without my confirmation... is that clear?"

"Perfectly, sir. Should I start immediately?"

"Yes, now," I replied, sitting down on the bed. He placed his gentle, human-like hand on my head, and stood staring off into space. Nanomachines spread from those fingertips through my skin and thence throughout my body, probing me and reporting back to the robot.

"You have a number of issues," it began, "the most significant being a cancer in your brain. It appears to be attached to the corpus calosum, but is interconnected to several places in both hemispheres. It poses a significant risk to your life, and should be removed."

"Listen carefully," I replied, suddenly sweating. "You may not remove the cancer. I believe it is providing me additional neurological functions."

"That is only remotely possible," replied the robot. "I'm not qualified to say either way."

"Can you make it benign without removing it or destroying its effectiveness?"

"I can render it benign. I cannot say if it will retain its effect."

"Do your best."

I was pretty nervous when the procedure was over, but as soon as I became intangible, I knew things were just fine. I laughed like it was the best joke I'd ever heard, and I was still laughing when I reappeared before the robot. It just stood there, incurious.

"Now, robot, I'd like to discuss my other issues, and then we'll talk about some upgrades."

When I was done with it, I returned the robot to the place and time I'd stolen it from. I used its built-in "warranty return" program to clear its memory... it remembered nothing about me afterward.

I was a new man when I got home. I knew I would lose weight and gain muscle mass over the next month, no matter what exercises I did or didn't do or how I ate. My senses were finely honed, and I could now see and hear and smell and taste well beyond the limits of normal human beings. My immune system was finely tuned and perfectly balanced; no modern germ could harm me.

For a week or more, I virtually forgot my time-traveling powers. I just lived, rejoicing in the new youth and strength that filled me. I was never so good when I was actually young. Yes, looking in your eyes, I see that you noticed.

Eventually, though, the lure of time returned, and I dived back in. I just wandered through the future, seeing how things developed. The world actually appeared to be getting better, a little bit at a time. It made me optimistic.

Then I ran off the end of the world. Just a little more than a century from my "present," the world was a smoking cinder. I quickly slipped backward, into the safe, comfortable world of just a decade earlier.

I found a quiet park and sat down. I was reeling from what I had seen. Nothing lived in that smoking ruin ten years ahead. What had happened? It took me a while to calm down, catch my breath... but then, time was no problem for me.

Eventually, I was ready to look again.

I moved forward nine years in a swift leap, then slowed, advancing at about an hour per second. All was well in the park for a few months, and then suddenly came a series of bright flashes. Then, ruin. I backed up and tried again, slowing to realtime but remaining intangible.

It was a war, and it came from space. I saw an alien ship falling swiftly, then stopping suddenly. Bolts and beams of light shot out from it, and people burned and died. It was horrific.

I watched over and over again, moving around the city to get different perspectives. I tried to watch it through the news media, sliding ghostlike into an apartment where I saw a news video playing, but the destruction fell so fast it didn't even make the news.

Finally I moved away from the destruction. I was shaken, no doubt. I couldn't go home, couldn't face my wife and children after what I'd seen. I had to take action. I had to save the world. I couldn't believe I was even thinking those words, but if not me, who else?

I didn't want to take any action that might change my past. To lose my family was unthinkable... so I had to start changing things sometime after the birth of my youngest child.

But I started earlier than that. I moved back another thirty years, and created a new identity for myself. It's not hard when you can move, intangible, through the halls of government. A birth certificate was easily created; school transcripts, work history, all fabricated.

I had less than a hundred dollars on my person, and I didn't want to return home until the future of Earth was saved, so that's all I started with. I bought a lottery ticket. Naturally, I could have matched all the numbers, but I chose not to... it would make me too conspicuous. What I took away from the lottery was still plenty, and I invested it very shrewdly.

My youngest was less than a year old when I made it to ten million. I began to invest with a plan, focusing on science and military technology. Soon I was able to take control of a few small contractors. Looking ahead, I discovered the great thinkers of the age by seeing their future works. I hired them, as many as I could, and I gave them all they could ever hope for... including, when necessary, hints from me.

Suggestions, really. I looked at their future works, their published articles which I collected from the future and then made sure that each researcher was pointed in the right direction. It didn't always work...

the creative mind doesn't always work that way... but when it didn't work so well, I was able to make further corrections. The pace of progress accelerated.

I encountered resistance, of course, as all captains of industry do. Within ten years I had a huge office building in a large city, running a company known by all. Bloggers and television commentators loved to talk about me, and they rarely had nice things to say. I was destroying the environment, accelerating global warming, and destabilizing the balance of power in the world.

They couldn't stop me. Criminal investigations fizzled out. Legislation restricting me never made it through Congress. I could always find a way to avoid being stopped. I was ruthless... I had to be. Someday, if the human race lived, we could fix all that I was destroying... but we had to live that long first.

Every so often I looked ahead, and each time I found things still ended the same way... with the world on fire. But eventually, it began to make a difference. Earth resisted the attack, for minutes at first, then for hours.

At last, I had lived in my other identity throughout the entire century, and I had made a difference. A tiny one.

Almost a week... Earth survived almost a week longer. From a quick death with little suffering to a terrible siege, a protracted death.

I had failed, but I did not give up. I took a step back and reviewed the inventions that my companies had created. Amazing things, really. We had conquered the solar system, putting bases on other planets and moons and in orbit here and there. Part of the solution to space travel was zero-point energy, which didn't work at all the way we expected, but it did work. Another part was artificial gravity, and antigravity. Yes, men could fly, wearing a simple harness controlled by the mind. We had created true artificial intelligence, and robots as smart as men but able to be specialized in ways men could not be. Cybernetic implants, nanotechnology, and genetic engineering had been married in the form of the new field of bioaugmentation. I was augmented myself, equipped with the ability to survive in vacuum without a spacesuit.

But there was one more thing... in the last days before the attack, we had finally created stable wormholes. Seeing that time was limited, I ordered the construction of a prototype wormhole generator in orbit around Jupiter just two months before the attack. It could form and maintain a very large number of microscopic wormholes, holding one end in a containment module while the other end could be carried around in a transport frame. On command, the generator end of a wormhole would be moved to the top of the truncated pyramid and opened, creating a spherical hole in space and time through which objects and people could move. The command could be delivered through the tiny wormhole itself, a fact which made the device an excellent remote-control transporter.

I ordered the construction of a small multi-wormhole transport frame, which I could carry on my belt. Out of the despair of the last days, I had conceived a new plan. If I couldn't stop the aliens on Earth, I'd have to follow them home.

I took a spacecraft back to Earth, then waited on a private space station until the day of the first attack. I became intangible, and slipped forward until the station was destroyed around me; then I moved backward, slowly, and followed the weapon back to the ship it came from.

Moving into the ship, I saw the alien destroyers of my world for the first time. I won't describe them, save to say that they were both strangely human-like and shockingly non-human. There were just a few aboard the ship, which was packed mostly with equipment.

Anchoring myself to the ship temporally, I began to run time backwards swiftly. The ship went back along its course, until it reached another world. Slowing my reverse progress, I looked at their monitors. I realized I was watching the destruction of another world progressing in reverse.

It was then that I began to call them the Xenophobes. It was obvious that they were on a tour of destruction through the galaxy, killing all life not like themselves. This made what I planned to do easier to contemplate.

I made time move backwards faster, and suddenly I found myself in a different place. Moving forward, I watched the ship I had been riding backward being built; I was on an alien space station. Remaining intangible, I sought out another ship, and rode it backwards the same way.

I lost count of the ships... they seemed to go on forever. But they became visibly less advanced, until at last I was riding on a chemically fueled rocket. I spent some time making myself familiar with that last, first world... the home of the Xenophobes.

In many ways their history was a lot like ours. They farmed, they built cities and villages, they married, they had children. They had war, too. Savage wars, as meaningless as any on Earth, but always ending in the losing side being exterminated.

Finally I felt I knew them well enough to proceed with my plan. I just didn't know if it would work.

I rode a wormhole back to the Solar System, back to the wormhole generator a week before the attack. I put my hands on the generator and extended my temporal field with all my power, and I made it disappear into time with me. Next, I synchronized myself to the Sun, and ran time backwards a day, taking the generator with me, depositing it beside its earlier self. Last, I used a wormhole, powered and controlled by the "later" generator, to transport the "earlier" generator to the Xenophobe world.

Yes, it's a paradox. It's also how time works for me. I can't explain it, not yet anyway.

I dropped it into the deepest part of their largest ocean, during a period when they were living in medieval squalor and killing each other with swords. Taking a wormhole in a transport frame, I traveled forward very, very fast; in a few seconds of my lifespan, I moved fifty thousand years forward. This put me beyond my own time, somewhere around the year three thousand.

Then I opened the wormhole, and the ocean began to gush through it, running down the "drain" of the ocean-bottom wormhole generator. As I watched, the industrialized Xenophobe world around me just evaporated, replaced by a parched wasteland. I knew then that my plan was working.

I fell back then, back to the medieval Xenophobes, and moved forward a year per second, watching their world die, the water rushing down that drain and into an empty future.

Xenocide. I was guilty of it. You could say, it was them or us, but that didn't make it any less a crime.

I thought it over for a while. Perhaps, if the Xenophobes were simply set back a ways... a hundred thousand years, perhaps... I could arrange for the human race to meet them on more even terms. Superior terms, even.

I used my power to spawn another wormhole generator, the same way I had before. I buried it inside a cave in a remote area of the Xenophobe world, covering the entire machine, exposing only the very peak where a wormhole might be opened. Then I took a wormhole forward with me, past the gushing spray of the ocean, forward until I found a time when the return of the water (and the sealife within it, of course) had resulted in the return of life to the world. I opened the wormhole within another cave, and stepped through it, back to the still-living medieval Xenophobe world.

I watched, a year per second, but they didn't find the escape hatch to the future. They still died.

Finally I used myself as bait. They couldn't resist trying to catch and kill me, and I led them on a merry chase across their world to the cave.

They had one last, horrific war then. I watched it. Perhaps one in a hundred Xenophobes made it into the wormhole, taking with them the simple implements and the animals and plants they would need to restart their civilization. I decided I had done enough... they could have all survived, if they hadn't insisted on fighting. They had time.

I stepped through a wormhole, back once again to the Solar System. I was eager to get back to my family... I had lived perhaps twenty years since I left them. But there was no one... other than the generator, there was no sign of any technology in Solar space.

Worried, I returned to Earth, under my own power. It took a long time, but I used my power over time to make it go more quickly for me. What I found on Earth astounded me.

There was no sign of the world I'd started from.

America was the sole domain of the Native Americans, who lived as they had hundreds of years earlier, before the white man came. Europe was likewise stunted, held at the level of the middle ages. I wondered if I had lost my place in time, but a London newspaper proved that I was, in fact, when I thought I was.

Then I saw them, for the first time. The aliens I call the Fuzzies. White furred, spider eyed, gentle creatures, armed with stunning weapons. I watched them arresting a man who had built a bicycle; they destroyed it with a blast from the sky, which my sensory implants identified as a particle beam.

I fell back in time, following them, until I found the day in the year 1242 when they first appeared. I watched as they placed the whole world, the whole human race, in a sort of protective custody.

They held us back. The progress, good or bad, that had led to my world now would never happen.

My family would never happen.

I realized that the Fuzzies must have been one of the races destroyed by the Xenophobes; removing one menace created a new one. I had to fix this too, it seemed.

I flew forward in time, until many thousands of years in the future, the human race finally rebelled against the Fuzzies. The new society was a decent one... thousands of years of rule by the Fuzzies had bred much hatred out of humanity. But I had just one mission... to restore my own timeline. It was a selfish mission, I knew, and many times I wondered if I had become something evil.

But I couldn't stop.

I moved through that future society, taking the many advancements they made into myself. I established a facility on the Xenophobe moon, placing another instance of my generator there, and populated it with robots loyal to me. It became a laboratory; any time I wanted to understand something, or reproduce something, I sent it there and gave the robots as long as it took. Time was never an obstacle.

I became something more than human, augmented in many ways, surrounded by an invisible cloud of nanobots linked to my neural implants. Wormhole-enabled sensors and communicators enabled me to expand my reach, my vision, as far as I wanted.

Finally I fell backward to 1242. I had what I needed... the technology to hold the Fuzzies at bay. To drive them away from my world, before they ever set foot on it... I knew there must be no trace of their influence to alter history again.

I spread my nanobots, my sensors and communicators, throughout the Solar System weeks before the Fuzzies would arrive. Powered off, they wouldn't be noticed.

I dressed myself in period clothes, on a whim, and set myself down in a wooded area near London. I activated a few of my sensors, monitoring space for the arrival of the Fuzzies; while I did so, I looked around the countryside. It had been a very long time since I had taken a walk.

I felt them as they crossed the orbit of Saturn. I walked out into a meadow, probably looking distracted, as in my mind I watched them approach.

But this time was different. Even as I saw them approaching, new spacecraft burst into Solar space, appearing from self-generated wormholes. New aliens I knew nothing about. I considered activating more of my sensors, but I decided not to. I would watch this play out from a distance, and after I knew what the new aliens wanted, I could always fall back again and stop them.

They placed themselves between the Fuzzies and Earth. I could hear their hails, even decode the messages the new aliens sent to the Fuzzy ships, since I had learned the Fuzzy language.

They told the Fuzzies to leave, and then they destroyed a Fuzzy ship like a man might swat a fly.

Sensibly, the Fuzzies left.

I felt the new aliens turn their attention to Earth, and I realized they were looking for me. I was the only variable which was different this time the Fuzzies came. It had to be me.

I played dumb, pretending to be an ordinary farmer, tending his sheep. When they landed, I tried to act overwhelmed.

They took me with as much care as you would pick up a kitten or a puppy. I was obviously valuable to them.

I spent a long time, making them teach me about themselves slowly. I somehow felt it was better if they thought I was a simple medieval farmer. Rather than teach me their language, several of them learned mine. They taught me things a medieval man wouldn't have known, like the fact that the Earth is round and revolves around the Sun, and I pretended not to believe it just long enough to keep them in the dark about my true level of knowledge. They also explained as much about genetics to me as they thought I could learn. It took a lot of time, but what was time to me?

Finally the day came when one of them, who called himself Zenal, explained the situation to me. "We are responsible for your power to travel in time," he said.

"How have you done this?" I asked.

"Many years ago our home world was destroyed in a natural disaster," he said. "For almost that long, we have searched for a way to retrieve our world. It is what we live for. Some of our scientists discovered that it was possible to travel in time, but even with our most powerful calculating machines we could not solve the formulas necessary to do it."

"And how does that involve me?"

"It involves your whole race," he replied. "Many years ago our scientists visited your world and changed your people so that, in the course of reproducing, the formulas might be solved by your genetics. We hoped that someday, a man of your people would be born with this power. At last it has happened. We knew how to detect the activation of the power, and as soon as we did we came here."

I protested my disbelief once again, then after some reassurances from Zenal I said "I see. So how can a single man, even one who is a master of the past and future, save your world?"

"We have created a device which can save it," he replied quickly. "You need only deliver it for us, moments before our world is destroyed. We have created a craft for you to ride in, small enough that you can carry it along with you by means of your power, and we have installed the device that will save our world within it. Simply take it then for us, and activate it; it will watch our world as it is about to die and will act at the last moment. The fires of space that destroyed our world will hide the disappearance of the planet so that our ancestors will believe it destroyed; otherwise, they might not take the actions that led to your powers, leading to a paradox."

I didn't tell Zenal that the paradox would probably be stable. I felt now that they were being honest with me, and I began to trust them, but to tell them how I had deceived them seemed a bad idea. So I held my peace and agreed to their plan.

The spacecraft they created for me was quite small, a sphere containing a seat within it. It seemed like a very simple machine, and it had no controls to speak of other than a large green button to activate the "device" he had described to me. It did have windows to look out of, and a telescope of sorts I could use to see their planet clearly.

Zenal explained the workings of the small ship to me several times, as one would explain a car to a Stone Age man; I chose to impress him with my understanding, rather than to drag out the proceedings any longer. He told me then that the large ship in which we were riding had arrived at the location where his world had been destroyed. Just like that, we were ready.

So I climbed into the small spacecraft, and they sealed the hatch and ejected it into open space. I stretched out with my powers and made the spaceship disappear into time with me.

It was easy enough to fall back until I saw their planet appear. Running time forward and back, I watched the planet being destroyed by a sort of wave of radiation. I could have just pushed the button, but before I did that, I wanted to know more about them, so I bailed out of the sealed spacecraft and did just that.

I descended to the planet by means of my antigravity implant, of course. I had already puzzled out much of their language, though like humans they had different languages in different places and eras. What I found, looking over their history, I understood... in many ways, the blue-tinged little humanoids were very much like humans. They had just expanded beyond their own solar system when the explosion of a strange wandering star destroyed their world; it had taken them a long time indeed to create me.

So I returned to the ship, as if nothing had happened, and I moved up to the moments before the destruction of their world, and at the appointed time I pushed the button. The device released a wormhole, much as I had expected, and I watched as long as I could without activating my beyond-human sensory abilities... I was concerned their little ship had recording devices that might detect them.

With my mission completed, I returned to Zenal's time, and his ship retrieved me just as he had explained. They thanked me then, Zenal in words and the others by means of awkwardly shaking my hand. The ship had a small crew, five individuals including Zenal, so it didn't take long.

"Return to the small craft, and we will place you safely on your own world," he said at last. "And once again, please accept our thanks for all you've done for us."

"It was my pleasure to help you," I replied, and then I turned and walked toward the small ship.

I felt the weapon as it entered my body.

It was tiny, no bigger than a speck of dust; no normal person would have noticed it, and I'm sure that's what they were counting on. But I was far from being a normal person.

I captured the tiny device a few inches up my nose, slipping it through a wormhole to the lab on the Xenophobe moon. I began to turn around; as I did so, I brought up my defenses, and I sensed six more of the tiny devices in the air around me. I sent them to the lab also. By means of another wormhole I received the lab's report, after twelve years of careful study; I scanned the "executive summary" and filed the rest for later. Evidently they were tiny bombs, any one of which could reduce my head to a paste.

I reached out to the microprobes I had scattered around the Solar System, awakening them, and it was then that I detected the warships. Six of them, in various positions. Each was a weapon, and each was different; the probes related to me that any one of them could wipe out all life on Earth. Some were massive, others quite small, but it seemed that each ship contained just two alien "crewmen."

I fired up my wormhole generators and began dumping the crews from the warships into the hold of the flagship. There were no weapons on board, according to my microscopic probes, save for the coffee-can sized device that was the source of the tiny bombs. I disabled it and sent it off to the Xenophobe moon, and then I wormholed the empty warships into orbit there also.

One point one two seconds had passed, and I was just completing my turn. I could see by their expressions that neither of my hosts knew what had just happened; how could they? But then a different expression passed over Zenal's alien face... he had just realized that things weren't going according to plan.

I looked at him, hoping he could read my expression of scorn. "I plundered endless futures that will never be for weapons of such power and subtlety that the Fuzzies would not dare to stand against me. You have no chance against me. I trusted you, I really did. I saved your homeworld. Is this, then, the thanks I get?"

"You do not understand," replied Zenal. "You are too dangerous. Your power, which saved my world, could condemn it just as easily. Your planet, your people, still contain the potential we put there. Even if you promise to do us no harm, how can we know that no other will arise there to threaten us?"

"You can't," I replied. "But know this: threaten my world again, and I will deal with you harshly. You cannot know this, but even before I saved your homeworld, I saved your people and mine from the species I call the Xenophobes. You've never met them, but someday you will... I went far back into their past, when they were still very primitive, and moved them entirely into the future. They would have killed you all, just as they were going to kill all of my people. Threaten the Earth again, and I'll deal with you in at least as decisive a fashion."

I turned away from them and walked past the tiny spacecraft they had given me. I didn't need it, of course; I had only used it so they wouldn't know what I was capable of. Now I wanted them to know. I pushed through the atmosphere-retaining field and stepped into open space.

When I was a few hundred meters from the ship I turned to watch as a wormhole swallowed it. It would arrive in orbit at the new location of their homeworld.

I turned my attention to the future then, moving forward, looking for further attacks, whether by them or others. For a thousand years, only the Puppet Masters, which I had come to call them, threatened the Earth; five times they tried to destroy it, and I stepped in each time and stopped them before they even got close. I decided that a thousand years was enough leeway for the moment; my thoughts turned then to my wife and children.

I became intangible, then took a wormhole to my home. I had lived most of seventy-five years since leaving, but I used that power which the Puppet Masters had given me to slide back in time to the day I left.

I watched, still intangible, as my earlier self got up that morning. I saw him leave, flashing black as he disappeared; I was careful, staying clear of him so he wouldn't detect me. Then I started to descend, ready to step back into my life. But then he returned, flashing black in front of me again.

That's when I realized my life had gotten away from me. Permanently.

Recall that on that first trip I found the world destroyed in less than a century, courtesy of the Xenophobes; but this version of me found only the relatively rosy future I had just created. He was me, but he wasn't, and there was no longer any room for me in the world.

I knew then what I had to do. I returned to the Xenophobe moon to formulate a plan; when I was ready, I slipped back to Earth, in the year 1999, where I released the tailored virus my lab had created. I chose a year that was after the birth of my last child, but before my cancer; the other me, the one who was living my life now, deserved his children, and I still loved them, so I avoided doing anything that could change the fact of their births.

A few people, out of the billions on Earth, died from the virus, but for most it was no worse than a cold. It didn't even make the news. But the genes contributed by the Puppet Masters all those millennia ago, the genes that gave me the power to travel in time, were gone when it had passed.

I went forward again to the time from which I had left and watched, immaterial, as I, that is, the other I, went through an entirely normal day. No time travel, no cancer. I went forward, following his life to its natural conclusion. All normal.

So here I am before you, telling you my story. I'm not what you'd call human anymore, but yet I am still a man. I miss my life, my friends, my family, but most of all I miss you. I waited until your husband was miles from here, but in a way he's right here in front of you. I remember our wedding, and the births of our children. I was there with you when your father passed away.

I needed to tell someone.

I'll leave you now. I have work to do. The whole human race is my job now, and I have big plans.

Maybe I'll come back some day and tell you all about it.

About the Author

Chris Gonnerman was born in rural northeast Missouri in 1965, and has spent most of his life there. While his work is in various computer-related fields, his passion for games and for writing led to the creation of the Basic Fantasy Role-Playing Game rules in 2006. He has always written science fiction and fantasy, but only recently decided to publish his work.

Contact him on Facebook:
www.facebook.com/chris.gonnerman

Find more books by him on Amazon.com:
amazon.com/author/chrisgonnerman

Printed in Great Britain
by Amazon